AULLY'S
JOURNAL

The Sequel to
Grandma Ida's Story

Aully's Journal
The Sequel to Grandma Ida's Story

Outskirts Press, Inc.
http://www.outskirtspress.com

ISBN: 978-1-4787-6690-2

Outskirts Press and the "OP" logo are trademarks belonging to Outskirts Press, Inc.

PRINTED IN THE UNITED STATES OF AMERICA

Contents

Introduction

Shannon and Charles have been married for many years. They had two sons and a daughter. Charlie the oldest, John, and a daughter they named Ally. The two boys had moved from the mountain and the ranch on the Grand Mesa a couple of years ago. Charlie was in his first year at the University in Fort Collins, and John had decided to go down valley to finish his last years of high school in Grand Junction staying with his Uncle Lars' family. Ally on the other hand loved the mountain and wanted to stay on the ranch. That suited both Shannon and Charles just fine. It was hard to see the boys leave, but it was obvious their hearts were not into ranching.

The boys each had their own rooms in this big house, where their bedrooms were located. It seemed like such a waste to keep them like a shrine. Shannon was restless and had to find a project to keep her busy. She had not done any writing since the book about Grandma Ida had gone on the bestseller list many years ago. She was not even sure she could write again. There did not seem to be anything she had felt as passionate about since Grandma Ida. She tried to write, even started a couple of manuscripts, but never finished them. Fiction just was not something she could sink her teeth into. She sent a few articles to the Denver Post and they had been received well, but nothing substantial. Her late boss had died six years ago and she never really cared to join the new reporters and editors. However, lately she knew she had to do something to keep her mind busy.

She had talked to Charles, asking him what he would think about her going to the Denver Post Newspaper where she had worked before. She thought she could get a job there maybe working a couple weeks a month. Charles was not in favor of that at all, but he could see she was restless. One day as he was rummaging through all the stuff in the attic, he decided to drag out the old trunk they had stored up there. Maude and Grandma Ida had their personal journals in them. Even a few of Aully's things were there, and he had not looked at them in many years. Even after they had died, he only just glanced at them then closed them. He felt they were to private and personal. After all these years, most of the people who were in those journals were all gone. He was sure both Maude and Grandma would not mind if Shannon looked at them.

With the help of one of the hired hands, he hauled the old trunk down stairs and told Shannon, "Honey, maybe this will give you some inspiration. I know you can write, you just need something to write about. I don't know what is in these journals, but Maude and Aully have a story to tell and I think they would be honored to have you write their story."

Next day Shannon had finished with all her normal household chores and was just sitting down to her morning cup of coffee. Glancing at the trunk sitting there in the middle of the living room she timidly walked next to it and gingerly opening the lid. The musty smell of age filled the room. Glancing inside she noticed old files and pictures. Lying on top of all these things was great grandpa Charles' old sweat stained hat. Next to it was the old Colt pistol that had belonged to Maude, still stuffed in the old holster she had always wore. The most noticeable thing that caught her eye was the journals that had been carefully tied together in blue ribbon and an old faded paper on the top that read "Aully."

Absentmindedly she had placed her coffee cup on the table in front of her. Lifting the bundle out of the trunk, she slowly sat down on the couch. She laid the bundle on the table. Slowly and gently, she brushed the dust away untying the ribbon and letting it fall to the sides. Carefully, she lifted the top journal out of its resting place and opened the cover.

Aully Samuel Lawson

Aully had left the Lawson Ranch in 1895, when he was not much more than 17 years old. He wanted to see the rest of the world, but more then anything he had wanted to be a mountain man. His story revealed a life of adventure in the west and the men who endure the hardships in their search for the riches and the promise of striking it rich in the gold fields, of the Yukon and Alaska. An era of bygone days that most people can only dream of. He was truly a man of the Rocky Mountains that civilization came too soon for.

In addition, among his belongings was a very delicate silk hankie with the words embroidered in the corner, "Maude and Aully." Securely kept in the first page of his journal, it had been wrapped very carefully in another silk fabric, and tied with a thin blue ribbon.

Shannon had found her story and could hardly wait to show these things to Charles. She needed a place to do her writing. The very next day she took all the furniture out of Charlie's bedroom and packed away all his trophies, even his cowboy boots were put in an old trunk to be taken up to the attic. In their place, she set up a desk for her computer, with a printer, file cabinet and a long spread table. She made sure she had a coffee pot and a small refrigerator so she would not be interrupted for any reason. She even had the telephone removed from the room. Shannon figured if anyone wanted to talk to her, they could leave a message and she would get back to them when she had time.

When Charles saw all she had done he was not surprised, but he was wondering if he would ever see her again. Then he grinned and walked away saying to himself, "You go girl."

Next morning Shannon opened the first of the many journals Aully had left behind. It was noon when Charles walked into the room with a tray and said, "Honey, I thought maybe you would like to have something to eat. You haven't left this room all morning." "Oh, Charles I am so sorry. You would not believe what I have been reading about this most fantastic man. I don't know where to start." Charles just looked at her and smiled saying, "Honey, I know you will find a way to tell his story. Just start at the beginning and put yourself in his life and it will all come to you."

"Start at the beginning." She thought for a moment then began to type. The words seemed to flow from her, filling the room with images of the Lawson ranch and the new frontier, the pine forests and snow covered mountains of the Canadian Rockies. A story that had been locked up in an old trunk for to many years was now going to be told.

Aully's Journals

Mamma had always told us kids we had to learn to read, write and learn our numbers. My greatest passion was to read everything I could get my hands on about the Mountain Men and the Fur Trappers. There was very little time to read while I was on the ranch. There was so much work to be done.

Every morning after the milking was done Daddy would have my older brother, Lars, take the cattle out and graze them in the hills for the day, then bring them back in time for the evening milking. When I got older and could handle the job I begged Daddy to let me go. Then I could practice my trapping and I would take one of Mamma's flat frying pans with me so I could practice panning for gold in the river, but I never found anything. I would not have known if I found a gold nugget, as I did not know what one even looked like.

I trapped for the muskrat, mink and beaver that we would take to town and trade for supplies. I became pretty good at it and this made Daddy happy with me, as I was helping to make the much needed money to run a ranch this size. He was never able to except my passion for dreaming about the Mountain Men and how much I wanted to be one. I even took to dressing like the pictures I saw in the little dime novel books. He said I was a dreamer and he would yell at me and tell me to get my head out of the clouds.

I heard him say to Mamma one day that he was afraid I

would never make a very good farmer let alone a rancher, that maybe our son, Aully, was a bit simple minded. Mamma would scold Daddy, "Don't you say such a thing about our Aully. He may be a dreamer, but I remember a young man who was also a dreamer, dear husband," and that was how we happened to be here. I loved him anyway and I would have followed him to the moon if he had wanted to go there. "You let our boy dream all he wants to." She would lovingly look deep into Daddy's eyes with so much conviction he could not argue with her anymore. He just said, "I love my son with all my heart, but sometimes I wish he would pay more attention to his chores. I am just afraid one of these days he will leave and I won't have him with me anymore." Mamma said with sadness in her voice, "I would imagine that was exactly how our Mamma and Daddy felt as they waved for the last time, when we boarded the ship for Colorado, America, don't you think?"

Daddy just nodded saying almost in a whisper, "You are right." Then he kissed Mamma on the forehead and turned, walking away with his head down. Oh, how I loved Mamma that day. She understood so much more than anyone could imagine. I watched as she lifted her apron to dry the tears as they fell from her eyes.

In the spring of 1886, Mamma went into labor with my sister, Maude. It was a very hard labor and Mamma was so weak and tired after 16 hours. By the second day, Daddy was scared and the worry was beginning to show on his face. He had not slept at all. He would sit at her side holding her hand and then he would go sit at the kitchen table with his head in his hands and I could hear him crying, "Please God don't let her die." He was a strong man but he could not hold back the fear. The neighbors' wives would come to relieve him and to try to help Mamma. Many of their husbands would come and sit on our porch and wait with Daddy. They would take turns doing the chores so Daddy would not have to leave Mamma.

Mamma was getting so much weaker and we all prayed. I was so afraid as I walked out into the pasture and collapsing to my knees, I said a prayer to God. "I promise if you save my Momma and this little baby I will be the best brother a baby could ever want and I will spend my life taking care of it. Please God don't take my Mamma, we need her and Daddy would never be able to live without her." I am sure God must have heard me because within the next hour, we could hear Mamma scream, and at the same time, the cry of a baby could be heard. Then the most beautiful little baby girl made her appearance into this world. Lars, Daddy and I ran to the bedroom door at the same time, but Daddy pushed us aside and ran to Mamma tears rolling down his cheeks as he bent to kiss her face. Daddy was telling her how much he loved her and then he picked up the small bundle, turned around and laid her in my arms.

He said, "This is your little sister. She will be your responsibility to watch over and protect from this day forward." "God must plan to hold me to my promise," I thought to myself. Daddy told me, "Clean this little girl and I think you should be the one to name her."

I had never held anything so tiny before and I walked away tiptoeing afraid she would break if I made a noise. I did not even know how to hold her. Then I realized Daddy had said for me to wash her.

"How do you wash such a tiny thing like this?" I thought to

myself. I looked around to see if there was a safe place for me to lay her while, I got the water and whatever else I needed prepared. Then I saw the clothesbasket that still had the clothes in it from the clothesline Mamma had just taken down, so I laid the baby in it. Then began the task of getting warm water and some of the little nighties mamma had made for her. I knew I would have to figure out the diapers too.

I filled the washbasin with warm water testing it with my elbow to make sure it was not too hot. As I placed her naked little body on a blanket on the table, I did my best to clean all the blood and messy fluids from her body. There was a cord on her tummy that had a string tied to it. I did not know what to do with that so I just carefully placed it against her tummy. I dressed her in the pink gown Mamma had made, and then I wrapped her in a blanket and lifted her into my arms. Before I took her back to Mamma, I remembered Daddy had said it would be up to me to name her. I had seen a name in one of my dime novels that I had liked. When Daddy asked me what name I had picked out I told them, "I think she should be called "Maude. "It was the name of a princess." Mamma smiled a weak smile and said, "That would be a very nice name to call our special little girl."

Maude Marie Lawson was the name Daddy wrote in the family bible. All the family names were written in the family Bible, Momma had brought from Sweden. It dated back to our very old ancestors. I loved looking through the names written there and especially I liked seeing my own name written there. Aully Samuel Lawson, born 1878 on the John and Ingabar Lawson Homestead, in Colorado, America.

Maude would follow me everywhere I went; she was like

my shadow. Often times as I would be saddling my horse to go do my chores she would be kneeling and gazing at me from under the horse's belly. "Where Aully going?" she would ask. Of course, she knew the answer, but she just had to ask anyway. It was a game with us and she would giggle when I would answer, "To the moon."

"How you get there?" Maude would ask. Answering her I would say, "I will ride to the end of the rainbow and then I will jump onto the colors and follow them to the moon." With those big dark eyes wide with wonder, she would beg me to take her with me.

I would tell her, "You are too little and the clouds would swallow you up and you would get lost." She would run back to mamma and tell her "Aully scare me." Mamma would laugh and hug her and say, "Aully was just teasing you, and then she would say with a giggle, "Aully cannot ride a rainbow it's to slippery."

I always loved the time when I could go back to the hills with the cattle, following behind them as they made their way through the pines to the very the edge of the mountains.

Looking off into the distance, I could see the ranch far below and feel like I was on top of the world. Many times, I would give my pony his freedom, as he would mingle among the cattle. Most times the huge elk would be grazing with the cattle as if they belonged.

I would play a game with them as I slowly urged my horse to move close enough for me to reach out, touching their huge antlers. The big Bull Elk would just shake his head and stare at me with those black eyes and then he would lower his head and continue to eat the sweet grass. One special day as I rode close to one of the Bulls, reaching out to touch his huge rack of horns, I suddenly became aware that I was not alone.

I slowly sat up in my saddle and turned to see the most magnificent dark skinned Indian just at the edge of the tree line sitting tall on the back of a beautiful black Stallion. He was watching me with a slight smile and then he smiled nodding as if to say hello. I had never seen anyone like him before. Occasionally, I would see a Ute Indian, but this one was not a Ute. I was not sure what he was, "maybe a Cheyenne", I thought to myself. He was bare from the waist up and his legs were bare. He had on leather leggings that came up to his knees with long leather straps that hung loose. The intricate beadwork appeared to be special made just for him and covered the front and over the toes of his moccasins. His hair hung to his waist, tied back with leather straps. Braided through his hair were eagle feathers, which the wind blew around his shoulders and into his face.

I could not help but notice the bow and a quiver of arrows that hung over his back. Strapped to his waist was a large knife in a scabbard and a pouch. Draped over the back of the Stallion was a colorful woven blanket, which he was sitting on. At once, I knew he was no ordinary Indian. "What was he doing here?" I thought to myself. I do not know why I was not afraid, but I was more in awe of him then anything. He was magnificent to look at on his Big Stallion. Together they were a remarkable sight.

At first, we just looked at each other then he moved closer stopping just in front of me. Neither of us spoke at first, and then he spoke in a language I was not familiar with. I knew some Ute from the times Chief Ouray would come to our house and visited with my father, but this was not the Ute language. As he realized I could not understand him he began to speak in very careful English, and using sign language as well. "I have watched you before in these mountains and believe you have the heart of the great Elk and are one with the mountains. I will call you, "Boy who touches Elk." "I have seen a vision of you and I see a great adventure that awaits you. There will be many challenges you will have to face before you return to these mountains. A new life in the far northern country of the ice and snow awaits you, where the Raven will follow you."

He raised his hand and then he turned disappearing into the forest. I did not even get to speak or ask him who he was or where he came from. He would haunt my dreams for many years after that. "What did he mean I would have many adventures and challenges before I returned here?"

I never spoke of him to anyone but I could hardly wait to go to the grazing land with the cows, hoping to see him again. He never came back. That was when I made a vow that if I had to I would search for him if I had to search under every rock and look in every canyon in these entire Rocky Mountains.

I would hear rumors of a great Chief, who wandered these mountains, but no one really knew too much about him and only a few had ever seen him. They all agreed that he was rumored to be a very powerful chief of the Blackfoot Confederacy from the northern plains of the Canadian Territory. His name was Chief Black Raven, a powerful medicine man and a very important visionary Chief among the "People". He had many visions of the dangers that were to come to his people. He had made many warnings for them, but they would not listen. It made me wonder even more about what this Chief Black

Raven had said about my future and why I had come to him in his vision. "What did all this mean, and why was he so far from the Northern Territory of Canada?" I wondered what he meant when he said, "The Raven would follow me?"

By the time, I was 16 years old, I could stand it no longer, so I went to Mamma and Daddy telling them that I wanted to go and see the rest of the world, that I was not happy on the ranch anymore. They tried to talk me out of it but I was determined.

Daddy told me he needed me for the spring round up to help drive the cattle to the railroad early in the spring, and then if I still felt the same he would not stop me. My dear Maude was the one I hated to leave. When I told her of my plans, she cried in my arms and begged me not to go. After I explained how I felt she very reluctantly said she understood, that although she never wanted to leave the ranch she would wait for me to come back.

Spring was a long time in coming. The weeks dragged as I counted the days to the roundup. All the ranchers gathered their cattle and after the branding, the cowboys drove the cattle to the valley stockyards in Grand Junction. Now I could finally say I had done what I promised Daddy. At last, I was free to follow my dream.

Deep down inside I knew Daddy had hoped I would change my mind and forget all those things, but there was no persuading me otherwise. Daddy had picked out the best horse on the ranch. Buddy, was the best and most dependable riding-packhorse of all the horses on the mountain which was a good thing. His level head saved me many times. My Stallion Jake was also the best horse on the mountain. I owed my life to him.

Mamma had packed me all the food and blankets she could possibly put together for my trip. "Just in case something happened and I would need them, like a blizzard;" she would say. It was early spring and not likely to be a blizzard. It made her feel better, so I did not argue. She had packed extra-long underwear and good wool socks. I did have to make her stop finally; by telling her, she was going to break poor Buddy's back with all this stuff.

As I was saddling my big bay stallion, Jake, Maude walked out to me, and as she leaned over his back in a voice weak from crying she said, "Aully I have something for you to take so you won't forget me." I thought to myself, "As If I ever could." She handed me a little white linen hankie that she had embroidered all around the edge with white lace. On the one corner, she had sewn "Aully and Maude 1895". It was wrapped very carefully in another blue linen cloth. I kissed her and put it in my shirt pocket telling her I would always carry it close to my heart. Then I stepped into the stirrup and turned Jake and Buddy towards the western mountains. As I glanced back for the last time at the home where I had lived for the last 17 years, I saw Mamma following me to the river's edge. She was crying and holding her apron to her face. I told myself I would come back, but for now I had to follow my dream to be a Mountain Man

I was to learn being a mountain man was not always as romantic as I had envisioned. Weeks would pass and at first, the mountains were just another camping trip. I knew all about that. Loneliness would creep into my heart at times as I missed the warmth and comfort of our little house on the ranch and the laughter as we sat in front of the big fireplace. However, as the food started to run out and the weather started to have the chill of fall, it was a time of hunger and cold as the early winter winds and snow took on a life of their own. I just could not seem to get warm. There were days when I would just stay in my makeshift shelter and try to stay close to the little fire I had built out of the wet wood. Most times, it would be more smoke than flames.

I had noticed the other trappers would take their furs into the trading post and trade for supplies. I had some good furs but I was not much of a bargainer for the trade goods. So many times I would be cheated out of their worth. I would say something about that, but the trader would just laugh and say, "Oh, alright I will give you a bit more only because I feel sorry for you," but it was obvious he was just out for the money and the furs. I was too desperate to argue.

The other trappers would laugh at me when they saw how amateur I was and how few furs I had to trade. My furs were not very well prepared and they did not look to good, but I did the best I could. At first, I did not realize I was being cheated.

Then one day after I had been trying to barter with the trading post operator and getting nowhere, there was a commotion in the back of the room as a big hairy man who looked like a giant to me stepped up to the counter and grabbed the clerk by his shirt collar. He told him in a raspy deep voice, very convincing, and loud enough to get everyone's attention, "I have been watching you and how you are cheating this boy. I have seen enough and I will cut your cheating tongue out if you do not start giving the 'Kid" his fair share, do I make myself clear?" He spoke all this in one breath. Everyone in the room had always given this man a very wide birth. They had seen his fury on many occasions when he got mad. He was no one to mess with. Then he threw the clerk against the wall behind the counter and stepped back.

I had seen this man before, but he always sat away from anyone else, preferring to be left alone and observing every one from a distance. I found out later that he was called, "Grizzly." A name well suited for him. He looked like a huge grizzly bear with his wild frizzled hair that hung long and below his shoulders, and his beard slightly streaked with the gray of age.

He was wearing a black grizzly bear fur coat and he smelt as if he had just killed it, as it had just stepped out of "It's" den. There was no doubt he was the true epitome of the mountain man. I was in awe of him and could not stop staring. He did not have any friends and obviously did not have any need for them, but everyone respected him and would step aside as not to anger him in any way. They all knew he could not tolerate anyone being taken advantage of and he would be the first to make it known.

When Grizzly turned to look at me he spoke just a few words, but they would be the words I would learn to live by. "If you want to be a mountain man you had better get tough and quit being a sucker. No one here likes you and you have no friends. If you cannot stand up and fight for what you want and for what is right then you had better go home to Mamma and get out of these mountains. You will never make it as a Mountain Man. Then he turned, grabbed his gear, and walked out the door. I just stood there paralyzed. For just a few minutes, there was silence in the post. As I lowered my head feeling shame and embarrassed I realized he was right. I looked up and looked that clerk straight in the eye. I was determined no one would ever laugh at me again. I turned looking at those men who had been laughing at me and were watching this episode as it unfolded. Then I said very confidently, "My name is Aully Lawson, and don't any of you forget it. Do not be fooled by my size or my youth. I have a good rifle and I damn well know how to use it. I will part your hair down the middle if I ever hear any of you laugh at me again."

"Now, Mister Trader, what did you say you would give me for my furs? In addition, make sure it is the same as everyone else is getting. If it is not, I will not hesitate to blow your head off. Do I make myself clear?" I was handed a pile of money, which, the trader did not bother to even count. Then I backed out the door with it in hand and taking my gear I secured it on the back of Buddy and rode out of the range of the Post. Looking back to make sure no one was following, I thought I saw Grizzly off in the trees, but I could not be sure.

I had staked a claim to a part of the river I was sure there would be Beaver. There were many signs of beaver dams running about 300 yards all along the river. I spent the better part of three weeks setting and checking my traps. In the meantime, I had found a good spot up river from my trap line to build myself a small shelter. I was in the Canadian Territory where there were still plenty of Mink, Muskrat and Beaver to trap.

For the next couple of years I wandered the mountains trapping for the best furs and selling them to the trading post. As I trapped, I practiced and learned the art of cleaning the hides well enough to get a good price for them, when I would go to the trading post.

Moving along my trap lines one day, I had crested the ridge

of the mountain, and I could see a long plush, green valley below, where the river had created a deep wide gully. I looked for sign of other trappers, and not seeing any, I thought to myself, "Maybe I would move my camp down there where I could set many traps and build a cabin from the tall timbers, that grew along the river. I had wanted to get a good shelter built before the winter set in.

It was already late summer and I would have to hurry. There were plenty of game in this valley to last me for the next couple of winters and fortunately, for me there were no sign that there was anyone that had discovered it. I set out 12 traps along the riverbank and another set of eight traps for the mink I had spotted earlier.

Now it was time for me to start cutting the trees I would need for my cabin. I wanted it to be about 20 feet above the riverbank to keep it high above the flood waters from the winter melt off in the spring.

I made it a practice to rise before the sun came up, have my coffee and a jerky slab, then head out to my trap lines. Then about midmorning I would return to camp, have my breakfast, and then work on my cabin. By the end of October, the cabin was ready to move into. I had built a fireplace against one wall and cut some wood, piling it against the outside wall close enough to the door to get to in the event of a lot of snowfall this winter. I had a lot more to cut, but I figured I would have plenty of time. I hoped to do that before the first snow.

I had built a shed in the back of the cabin where I kept my furs. It was full of the skinned and dried furs ready to take to the trading post. I was feeling good with myself this morning as I started on my rounds to my traps.

However, this morning all the traps were empty. I had not noticed anyone around, but for the next week every time I went to my traps it was the same story, they were empty. After a week of this same story, I decided to set a trap for whatever or whoever had gotten into my lair. I set a bear trap at the base of a log where whatever it was would have to step over and invariably would step into the bear trap. It was set at about four feet from my trap lines. If anything were to walk close, they would step into the bear trap and not be able to get lose. I did not have long to wait. As I was fixing my evening meal, a couple of days later I heard the scream of something in distress, in the area of my trap. I knew I had caught something, but I did not recognize the sound.

I grabbed my rifle, running out the door in the direction of the yowling. I stopped in my tracks not believing what I was looking at. It was a small Indian boy not much older than 12 or 13 years old. His foot was caught in the jaws of my trap. As I approached him he was frantically trying to pry the jaws open, but he was not strong enough. In disbelief, I looked all around to see if he was alone, but it seemed as though there was no one around. I thought to myself, "Where did he come from and what was he doing with all the beaver he had stolen?" I started to walk towards him, but he was fighting with the trap on his leg. I had to assure him I was not here to hurt him. He was trying to be brave not letting me see the tears. As I talked to him in a soft voice trying to win his confidence, he let me pry the jaws apart far enough for him to pull his foot free.

This boy must have been used to hardships and knew how to cope with pain as he tried to stand and run, but he could not put any weight on his foot and fell. I reached to help him up, but he put up quite a fight. Finally, I just lost patience with him and socked him in the jaw; he went out like a light, slumping into my arms.

There was no problem carrying this boy. He was so thin, half-starved and weak. The fire in the fireplace was still burning, but I threw another log on to keep it going. The cabin was cozy warm when he finally came to. I had cleaned and dressed his wound, but as he tried to stand on his foot, he realized that it was a futile attempt at bravery. After looking at the bandages, he lay back on the bed looking at me as if to say, "Okay, what now?" I had to laugh at him, as He was putting up a very brave front. However, it was not funny and I realized what a mistake that was when I noticed him looking at the stew I had in my pot on the spit in the fireplace.

"Not even a thank you," I thought to myself feeling ashamed. Aloud I said, "Oh well, I just have more traps to set." I fixed a bowl of stew for him and for myself. I watched him eat as if he had not eaten in a week or more. I then set out to replace more of the empty traps, thinking to myself, "Now that he has his belly full he won't find it necessary to steal from me again."

By midday after I had reset all my traps, I was heading back to the cabin when the little runt appeared in front of me, but this time he had two women with him. One was just a skinny little girl, I guest about 10 or 11 years old. She looked to be a bit simple, but she was a little thing. The other woman was a bit older and I would not even guess how old she was, but I was guessing she was their mother and she was a very beautiful woman, but to young to have children as old as these two children were.

The boy tried to use hand sign to tell me about them, but

the mother was able to explain some in her broken English, that they were family. They had to escape from a trapper's camp over the mountains. They were trying to get back to their people along the Chitchaw Valley of the Blackfoot Tribe, in the Canadian Territory.

Three trappers had taken them while they were out hunting for small game for the tribe. When I asked them where were they camped they gestured by sign language, "They had a small shelter in the forest along the river. They had no way to trap for food and when "Little Toad" had seen my traps he didn't hesitate to take the beaver to bring for us to eat. He didn't mean to steal them, but we had no food," was the mother's reply. They also said they were afraid the trappers were still looking for them and they had to keep moving to stay away and out of sight. All they wanted was to get back to their people.

Winter was moving in fast and for sure, and I thought to myself, "I can't just send them out into these mountains to freeze to death. They would never make it back to their people. They would surely freeze or starve. They would never make it without help." That night they all stayed in the small cabin, and by morning, the snow covered the ground and it did not show sign of letting up.

I rose early and after stoking the fire getting the cabin warm again, I went outside to the barn where the horses were. I had built them a shelter so they could get out of the weather as well. I knew that without them I would also not make it through these times in the mountains. All the time I was wondering what I was going to do about my new tenants. I had not figured three more mouths to feed.

As I headed back to the cabin a thought came to me as I remembered Mamma and Daddy, "What would they have done in these circumstances?" I knew the answer to that question before I even had a chance to think about it anymore. I felt eager and excited about my decision, but then a thought came to me, "What would they think about my idea." I had better give this more thought and I would have to explain it very carefully. Would they think badly of me? They had already had a bad experience with trappers. The cabin would be too small for all of them." A plan was starting to grow in my head. Mamma would just say, "We will just have to build on another room."

I walked back into the cabin to find a nice fire in the fireplace and the last of the stew was sitting on the table waiting for me. I was motioned to sit and eat. I asked, "Have you had anything to eat?" They answered that they had. I asked them to all sit with me while I ate. That I had a proposition to talk to them about.

I then told them what I had been thinking about. I tried to explain it to them as simply as I could. I said, "I had wanted to build a bigger cabin with a separate bedroom and a storage space off to the side. If they would be willing to help me with that, I would let them stay here through the winter. That would also mean I would get help with my trap lines and gathering more firewood and we would need more meat and dried food for all of us. I think with each one of us doing our share we could very easily survive this winter very comfortably. Then when the spring thaws begin they could continue to go to their people, and I plan to go deeper into the Canadian Territory, and maybe look for gold. I hear it has been discovered somewhere near Dawson."

They did not take much time to think my proposition over, as Mother answered in her broken English, "I have been so worried how I was going to keep my children alive if we left now. I know we would all freeze and die. We will stay until the snow melts. We will do as you have asked of us and then we will go to the People of the Blackfoot Tribe. I said, "Good, then that is settled."

Tomorrow we will begin to cut more trees to build on to the cabin." I was relieved and happy for the company; I had spent these months alone and desperately needed the companionship of other people. I had been thinking a lot about the ranch, Mamma, Daddy, and my dear little sister, Maude.

Most of the time we had to communicate in sign language, but I would practice theirs and they would let me teach them mine. After a while, we were able to talk to each other and understand each other. I learned that the daughter's name was "Tapping Bird". She was called that because when she spoke it would sound like a woodpecker as it tapped on the forest trees. It was hard for me to understand most times. I just could not understand what she was saying, so we would use sign language to talk to each other. She was a plain looking little girl, but as sweet as she could be.

The mother's name was Little Running Water. She was so beautiful with her long black hair and her dark skin. She reminded me of someone, but I just could not place who it was. Little Toad was a skinny kid. I could see he was going to grow into a tall handsome warrior one day, but he was lighter skinned and I guessed he was a half-breed. He had the long black hair of his mother, but he did not have the high cheekbones that are so prevalent of the Northern Indian. I wondered about that, but it was not my business and I did not need to know.

For the next months, our little family had managed to cut down enough trees to build our addition onto the cabin large enough to accommodate all of us comfortably. I had decided to also build an underground storage cellar just off to the right of the cabin. I braced it on the inside with logs, made a door on the top, and covered it with sod.

I was becoming very wary of the more and more trappers and claim jumpers that were beginning to move into the territory. There had been a lot of talk about the gold prospectors who had heard of the gold strike along the rivers. A lot of them were just honest prospectors looking to strike it rich, but there were those who would steal from their own grandmother if it would benefit them.

I wanted to have a place out of sight to hide my furs and supplies that would not attract any attention. As we stood back and looked at the cabin admiring our workmanship, I had to smile and admired the cabin. I also had to laugh at the new family I had acquired. We looked at each other, nodding and laughing. That night we celebrated with fresh fish and Little Running Water; a name I had shortened to just Running Water, had dug up some wild turnips while Tapping Bird had gathered some wild blueberries. A meal fit for a King. Toad as he was called now and I had gathered wood until we had a good size stash of firewood for the winter. Tonight there would be a nice warm fire in the fireplace followed by a good meal. As I looked around the little room and at my new temporary family, I felt at peace. Thinking to my self, "Not exactly what I would have planned, but this is not bad. No, not bad at all."

As the weeks past, Running Water would teach me so

much about surviving in the wilderness, and Toad, I was to learn even at his young age, was an accomplished marksman with the bow and arrow. He showed me how to make a good strong bow and then we would look for just the right wood to make the arrows, as they had to be perfectly straight. We found the flint stone to make the arrowheads as well. We would go out on hunting expeditions together and hunt for the elk and deer with just the bow. Soon I was able to bag an elk and place the arrow in just the right spot to kill with just one arrow. It was much too valuable to use more and possibly lose one.

We would be gone for two to three days on these hunts. When we returned with our trophies, immediately, Running Water and Tapping Bird would skin and stretch the hides to dry while Toad and I would start the process of drying and preserving the meat. As a team, we worked very well together. We especially liked the strips of dried venison seasoned with the wild garlic that, Running Water had dried and ground into a fine powder, adding salt to taste. She let the strips of meat soak in brine for a couple of days and then dry in the sun. Later we would eat these strips as jerky or boiled with wild vegetables for a stew.

The hides were made into warm coats and long leggings for everyone. One time when we brought back beaver, Tapping Bird made warm hats for everyone out of them. She was a very good tailor and made warm hooded parkas for the four of us, sewing these all by hand. She said we needed them to keep the snow out and then she would smile. It was hard not to love this little girl.

Nothing was ever wasted; everything from the animals were dried and packed to keep dry or made into something.

The wild turnips and potatoes were buried in the dirt floor of the storage pit, later to be dug up for a delicious stew during the cold winter months. Berries were dried and placed in bags made from the intestines of the animals we brought home and hung from the ceiling beams.

Mamma had taught me how to make the sourdough brine to be stored in a waterproof container to be used for the bread and pancakes. We had gathered the maple syrup and had it stored in the containers that I picked up at the trading post. I had mixed it with some of the wild berries and boiled it together then strained it for a tasty juice.

For the next months everyone was content and happy as we worked together to make the best out of our situations. It was a long winter. By May, the sun was beginning to heat everything up and melt the snow. The Beaver were plentiful and we were able to yield quite a good cache to take to the Post.

My thoughts had begun to turn to the time when I would have to let Running Water and her children go. They had become so important in my life and I looked forward to seeing them first thing in the morning and the last ones at night. I could already feel the loneliness creeping into my heart.

I had become especially fond of Running Water in a way I had never expected myself to feel. I was not sure of how she felt about me. Nothing had ever been said between us about our feelings. I only knew I had made a promise to them that I would not hold them if they wanted to go.

One morning in early spring as I was saddling Jake and getting Buddy ready to go out on a hunt, Toad came to me and said he thought he would stay behind to check on the traps and check out the new line we had set. He said his mother would go in his place if that was okay with me. I thought that was a bit strange, as he always seemed excited to join me on these hunts, but I learned not to ever ask questions when they made up their minds. They always had a good reason for their way of doing things and it was always the best way in the end.

The horses were packed with enough supplies to last a few days. By the time, the sun was coming over the horizon Running Water and I were leaving and heading for the high country. We had spotted a huge Elk herd a couple of weeks before. Neither of us said anything for the next couple of hours. We just rode looking for signs of game.

Running Water rode up next to me and touched my arm indicating a covey of grouse. She signed she would see if she could snare a couple for our supper. I nodded and continued to ride on. By late afternoon, we had bagged two deer and had them gutted and placed on the makeshift sled Running Water had constructed. We decided to stop for the night and after we had made camp, I proceeded to hang our meat high in a tree and packed their stomachs with snow to keep them cold.

Running Water had a fire going and the grouse already on the spit. We did not talk while we ate, both of us just staring into the fire. I was feeling the tenseness and uneasiness between us that I had not felt before. Out of the corner of my eye, I could feel her watching me with questions on her face, but she did not say a word.

We cleaned everything up and repacked the sled for our early morning departure. As I crouched tying the last of the bundles Running Water walked up behind me, touching my shoulder, she tugged me to turn around. As I stood turning to face her, she loosened the tie on her buckskin dress; it fell to the ground revealing her naked body. I could not breathe as I looked at her dark skin with her long black hair blowing around her shoulders. Her breast rose and fell as she breathed. Then she took my hands placing them on her breast. The cold had made her nipples hard. I moved my thumbs over them and caressed her so gently. She unlaced the tie on my shirt, exposing my bare chest.

I reached for her, lifting her up as she wrapped her legs around my hips. Kissing her nipples caressing them slowly with my tongue, she sighed, leaning back. And then she lowered herself, intentionally sliding her soft skin over my body as she did. My body responded as she took my hand and beckoned me to lie down with her. We were unaware of the cold night as I pulled her soft warm body close to mine, crushing her breast against me. My hands felt hot as they moved over her smooth skin. I pulled her hips tight against my aching body, and she came to me with trembling eagerness. We were as one letting the heat of our passion explode, moving in rhythm together.

Our desire exploded as one frantic uncontrollable fire. My fever rose, exploding as I let all my pent up desire reach it's peak, forgetting even the slightest motion of her willing warmth. I could not stop. I gave her all of me in one hard thrust.

As we lay there afterward our passion spent, not letting go of each other and for many minutes, there was silence. Nothing needed to be said. I held her in my arms pulling the Bear Skin robe over us; we drifted off into a dreamless sleep of contentment.

As the sun was just cresting over the darkened sky. Unaware of the light rain that had begun to fall we could not contain our desire, again giving into our passion once more, remembering the fire of the night before, not able to let it go, each time our lips met our passion would explode like the fire of so many volcanoes we couldn't put out. We explored every part of each other's body, touching, caressing, and letting our lips kiss each new discovery. Finally, as we reached our climax, we lay wet in each other's arms not wanting these moments to end.

The rest of this hunting trip was a time of passion. Our hunger could not be satisfied. Every time we touched, our desire would take control. This time Running Water road behind me, on Jake, not wanting to be apart, with her arms around my waist, she would touch me sending a flame of fire through my loins, as she reached for the ties on my pants.

The last night as we prepared our evening meal, I wondered how we were going to tell Toad and Tapping Bird. As I looked at Running Water, she smiled knowing what I was thinking. She said, "Toad had planned that I was to come with you on this trip. He already knew of our feelings." Feeling foolish, I smiled and answered, "He is a very smart boy. Because I was afraid, I already knew how I felt, but I didn't know about you." "Do you know now?" She asked laughing.

By midday, we were heading back to the cabin, and just as we crested the Ridge, we both saw the black smoke, billowing up from where the cabin stood. Fear gripped me as I kicked Jake into a Gallup, grabbing my rifle at the same time. Running Water cut the line to the sled she was dragging and was riding Buddy hard at my heels. I had my rifle out of its scabbard and it was ready when I galloped in site of the burning cabin.

I could see Toad lying in a puddle of blood on the ground in front of the cabin. "Where is Tapping Bird?" I thought to myself afraid to think of the possibilities. By now, Running Water had reached Toad on the ground and then she turned and started to run for the house, crying, "Tapping Bird!" I grabbed her before she could go into the burning cabin, holding her while she fought to get out of my grip. I spoke to her in a hushed voice. "It is too late. Toad needs you now, he is still alive." She slumped for just an instant then she turned to look at him. As I let go of her she ran to his side.

He was hurt bad, but he was able to tell us in a weak voice what happened. "Three trappers came. I think I killed one with my arrow." Then he remembered, and asked, "Tapping Bird." Is she alright?" Then he passed out. I was able to put part of the fire out and saved half of the cabin, but the rest was too burned to save. I slowly went inside and found what was left of Tapping Bird's body, but it was so badly burned she was beyond recognition.

Running Water, even though I begged her not to go inside was determined, she was unconsolable as she dropped to her knees crying. She was chanting the death chant and rocking back and forth. There was nothing I could do for her; she did not even know I was there. She sang the songs of her people, the chants of the Blackfoot confederacy. I carried Toad into what was left of the unburned part of the cabin and after checking his wounds, I discovered that most of the blood on him and on the ground was not his. It must have belonged to one of the trappers. He did say he thought he had killed one of them.

When Running Water had finished with her chants, she came to me. Her eyes were filled with grief; they no longer had any sign of the love and passion we had shared just a few hours ago. They were filled with hate for the trappers who had done such a heinous thing to her beloved little girl. She only wanted revenge and to kill these animals. "But first I told her, "We have to bury our beloved little girl and we needed to tend to our son." She acknowledged what I was saying. She nodded and then she said, "I will go and search for them. We will get our revenge for Tapping Bird." I took her by the shoulders and said, "We will go find them together and I promise we will take our revenge." We must be smart and take all the time we need to find them. They are also smart and have been able to avoid being caught for a long time. We will be prepared when we find them."

Grizzly

As the days past, Toad was getting stronger and was able to tell what had happened. He said, "I went out to check the trap line and had only been gone for about 2 hours when I heard a faint scream in the distance. At first, I thought it was just a bird, but when I heard it again I realized it was coming from the cabin. I dropped my traps and ran for the cabin. By the time I got there, I could see Tapping Bird lying in the doorway. There were three trappers and one of them was dragging Tapping Bird back into the cabin by her feet. She was clinging to the doorframe crying, trying to stop what was about to happen. The trapper was drunk and laughing, saying, "She sure is a feisty little thing. I am going to enjoy taming this little filly."

"The other two trappers were watching this, laughing and sharing the bottle of Whiskey they had been passing back and forth. They were also very drunk. Tapping Bird looked up just as the trapper was able to pull her loose from the door. Then she saw me and screamed my name just as I ran into the clearing." He had to stop talking for a moment as he placed his face in his hands crying, "Those were the last words I heard her say."

Then he continued," Both of the men who were watching this scene turned to see me as one of my arrows hit the shorter one in the leg. I quickly laced another arrow into my bow, letting it go, hitting the other one in the shoulder. By now, they realized they had to stop me. The taller one got to me first and before he hit me with the rifle butt I got a good look at his face, then I blacked out. They must have thought they had killed me. They were more concerned about their own wounds. As I was regaining my senses, I was still unable to move or to get back on my feet."

"They yelled at their partner to come on, but he didn't hear them. "I heard one say, "To Hell with him. Let's go." He finally came to the door fastening his pants as he walked and then he picked up one of our lanterns and threw it into the house, throwing a lighted match after it. The flame exploded. I was not able to get up, but I did get a good look at him. He had a scar on his face from the side of his mouth to his ear, making him look like he was smiling."

"His eyes were big black and mean looking, with heavy thick eyebrows. I will never forget that face. He was a Half Breed. I would guess him to be half buffalo Indian and half Indian, not from this area, probably one of the southern Indians from Mexico. His hair curly, kinky and dirty, hung below his shoulders. He was wearing a long bearskin coat that was as dirty as he was. I could almost smell the foul odor of him from where I lay."

I had heard of the Half Breed they said was crazy. He killed just for the pleasure of it. I noticed the scalps hanging from his saddle horn. Then he mounted his horse, sinking his spurs into his ribs he rode after his buddies. He didn't even look at me," Toad continued. "He pushed the other two trappers aside and as they had to slow their pace to let him pass, it gave me just enough time to lace another arrow into my bow, I aimed carefully, hitting the tall one in the center of his back. I saw him slump in his saddle as he kicked his horse and rode into the forest after the other two and disappeared. I tried to crawl to the cabin but darkness overcame me."

"The next thing I remembered was you touching me. Tapping Bird never came to the door again. I could not help her. I will never forgive myself. I just pray to the Great Spirit to some day let me avenge her death and let me cut the heart out of this monster." Both Running Water and I tried to tell him there was nothing he could have done. She was already gone and you both would have been killed."There was no consoling him as he sobbed. The only thing he really heard was that her death would be avenged. That was when he looked up and said, "He will be mine to avenge for my sister's death." "There would be no question about that, if it takes me the rest of my life, I will find him," he said with deep conviction.

In the next week as Toad was quickly regaining his strength he had become sullen and quiet. He had become a man with a purpose. I knew we had to take our furs to the trading post and get more supplies. There was much to do with burying what there was left of Tapping Bird's body. Running Water wrapped her in a bearskin rug tying it tight with leather straps. As we lay her in her new resting place, no one spoke and no one worked that day as Running Bird and Toad sang the songs of burial. I stood in the distance and watched, my heart was heavy with grief for the loss of this very dear little girl.

The Next morning I rode into the forest looking for any sign of which way the trappers had gone. Following the blood droppings along their trail, I rode another six miles from the cabin, finding the body of the tall trapper. Toad's arrow lay to one side. There was a bullet hole in the middle of the dead man's forehead. He had been stripped naked of all his clothes and anything of value was gone. The animals had done the rest, leaving not much left to identify him. As I walked around looking for more signs, Jake raised his head, looking off into the distance. He sounded his neigh and receiving a reply; he lowered his head and pawed the ground.

I rode in the direction of the sound and found the spotted mare tangled in the brush, the saddle still on her back. If there had been any furs, they were already gone. The trappers had left her to die. After I got her untangled, I checked her over to make sure she was okay. I looped a rope around her neck and led her back to the cabin. I figured we could use her as a packhorse for our furs to take to the trading post. After that, she would make a good pony for Running Water.

Next morning we were packed with all the furs we had hidden in our storage cellar. We also had all the dried meat and dried berries packed. Running Water rode behind me, on Jake, her arms wrapped around my chest as I held her hands close to me. Candy, the name I had given the pony was packed with as much as we could get on her and Buddy was packed, leaving enough room for Toad. We did not leave anything behind and we made sure there would be no sign of life here. It was a solemn caravan as we left the home we had loved. We rode along the river's edge for the last time. The air was thick from the smell of the burning remains of our cabin and the spirit of sweet Tapping Bird resting amid the tall pines. No one looked back as we headed North in the direction of the trading post.

The going was slow as we climbed along the narrow path to the ridge reaching the summit where the waterfall cascaded 50 feet below to the river. We continued to follow the tall pines that shadowed the long valley beyond the river's edge.

The shadows were growing long when we finally stopped to make camp for the night. No one had hardly spoken all day, each in our own thoughts when I finally said, "We should plan to stay here for a couple of days to let the horses rest and graze. They have been carrying a heavy load and need their rest. We do not want to wear them out. We will need them to be in shape for the rest of our journey."Toad started to protest, but from the look I gave him, nodding towards his mother, he soon agreed. Saying, "Without our horses we will not make it, but when we get there we will ask about the dark trapper with the scar on his face. I am sure someone will know him." I answered, "He would not be likely forgotten if anyone had ever seen him. Don't worry, Toad, your time will come and you will get your revenge but we must be smart and not do something to warn him we are after him. We must plan our attack on our own terms," I pointed out to him.

Understanding he nodded and agreed. "They think it was just you and Tapping Bird, and leaving you for dead. They have no Idea about Running Water and me." Running Water had already started a fire for the evening meal. The packs were placed close by. The horses had already been hobbled and allowed to graze in the tall grass.

As they settled down for the night, Running Water cuddled close to me. I put my arms tightly around her hoping the warmth of my body would let my love comfort her. She cried silently against me. I stared up at the night sky wondering what we would do if we should encounter the dark skinned man. I shuddered at the thought, but Running Water understood my thoughts and whispered, "We will face it when the time is right. We will face it together."

I had learned to listen to her words of wisdom knowing she knew before things happened what she would do. Most always, she was right and this time I had to believe in her. I pulled her closer and drifted into a sad sleep, as I was also very tired. For the next five days, we traveled following the river and heading deeper into the Canadian Wilderness.

We felt a feeling of relief when we finally found the well-used trail to the Trading Post. Although there was still that feeling of foreboding I just couldn't lose. I reined in Jake and told them to stay put while I checked out who might be in the post before they brought all the furs in. Toad rode up next to me and said, "I don't recognize any of the horses."

I decided maybe I was being a bit cautious, but I still insisted they stay mounted. I had learned not to trust anyone. There were two trappers standing outside leaning against the wall eyeing us with suspicion, but made no move towards us

I lowered myself from the Stallion and handed Running Water my reins. I patted her leg and as I did so, I stepped onto the porch and opened the door. The smell of tobacco smoke and sweaty bodies was overwhelming. Every eye was on me as I walked up to the counter where the skinny, smelly, trader was looking over the furs of another trapper , telling him his furs weren't very good, and he wouldn't give him a cent more than he could get for them. They argued about how there were not very many good beaver in the rivers and they had all been trapped. The trader told him that was not his problem. In the end the trapper took whatever he could get for them, walking away saying loud enough for everyone to hear, "The cheating bastard." Everyone nodding in agreement.

All eyes were on me as I walked up to the counter. "What

can I do for you, now," The trader asked. "I haven't seen you here before," he continued. "Where you from?" I ignored his question. "I have some furs I need to trade for supplies." "Okay, where are they?" he asked. I turned and said, "I will get them."

I went outside and started to take the packs off Candy and Buddy, telling Toad and Running Water to follow close behind me. As we entered with our huge cache of pelts, Toad stopped at the door, stepping to the side and waited with his Rifle in his hand. At that time, the trader looked up, and seeing my companions, he said in a loud nasty voice, "We don't allow those dirty Indians in here."

I was immediately in a rage and grabbed him by the neck in a choke hold with one hand and held my pistol to his head with the other, saying in a low voice, "This is my wife and son and I don't give a damn what your rules are. You will treat them with the respect they deserve. They have earned it. You will also not try to dicker with me about price. These are prime furs and hides and I expect the highest price going for them. Do we understand each other? I don't have time or the patience for your Bull Shit."

The Trader could tell I meant every word I said. The trader raised his arms and said in a shaky voice, "Take it easy, I don't want any trouble here. I just meant we do not allow most Indians in here. But we do make exception to families." He then reached for the fur on the counter in front of him and began to inspect them. "These are nice pelts. Where did you get them?" I just stared at him not answering. He then said after looking at me, "It doesn't matter. I don't need to know." Then he noticed the marking on the inside corner. Three side-by-side wavy lines, meaning Running Water.

"Are these your wife's marks?" "Yes. They mean Running Water, her name. It also means if you ever see anyone other than her, my son, Toad, or me bring them in here they have been stolen. Just shoot them or let me know and I will."

Some of the other trappers stood and wanted to get a look at the mark and the furs, but after I looked at them, it was obvious I was not here to be friendly. They sat back down. I indicated we would need a lot more bullets, flour, salt, and coffee. I then indicated to Running Water to pick out whatever else we needed. The other trappers watched her and were in awe of her beauty. They nodded and stepped aside when she came close. Toad stood at the door with his rifle ready in case there would be any trouble. By now, there was no indication of any trouble. They were just curious. They had never seen the likes of us and the two Indians were not from this area they could see. These two were different, possibly Blackfoot, very distinguished looking. It was well known they were also known for their fighting prowess and horsemanship.

It was obvious to all of the trappers this mountain man was neither a "Cheechako," the name given to a new trapper by the Indians; meaning a newcomer. Nor was he a sourdough, (Someone who had been in the wilderness for many years and had lived off the land.) He was an educated, distinguished trapper who demanded respect and got it as soon as he spoke. The trader asked me my name. I told him it was, Aully and that was all the information I would offer. I had noticed a repeating rifle hanging on the wall behind the counter, and asked, "How much? Do you have bullets for it?" I asked the trader. He replied, "That is one of the new American Winchester repeating rifles."

"The American soldiers use them to fight the American Indians of the western plains of Wyoming and Montana Territory. No offense intended ma'am," he said looked at Running Water. She just stared at him with no expression. "I know what it is. I just want to know how much you are asking for it." "Well, I wasn't planning to sell it," was his reply.

"But, for the right price I could be persuaded." Then he slowly, cautiously, almost in a whisper said, "$50 bucks" and stepped back as he waited for the great explosion. I looked at him and said, "I will give you $25.00," daring him to refuse me. The gun and four boxes of shells were then added to my supply list. As Running Water and Toad took all the supplies out and packed them on the horses, I turned to the trader and said, "I have a couple of more questions for you before I leave. Do you have another horse I can buy?" After which the trader said, "There is a pretty good pack mule that was left here by some prospector who died."

"Also," I continued, "have you had a half breed Negro with a scar on his face come through here recently?" The room became deathly quiet as all eyes were on me. No one said a word and then a loud deep voice from the back of the room broke the silence. A huge man dressed in a bearskin coat stood. He had been sitting in the darkened corner of the room watching all that was happening. He said, "No one talks of that man. Everyone makes a wide berth whenever he is in the vicinity and no one here has the guts to face him, and if you are smart neither will you.

He is crazy and will kill anyone who gets in his way, just for the fun of it." I had to smile as I recognized Grizzly. "Hello Grizzly." "It is too late for that, and I plan to kill him." Grizzly walked to the counter where I was standing and after looking me up and down he said, "Well, I'll be damned. Hello Kid." "You have come a long way. Then he continued, "If you plan to confront this monster you had better be prepared to die doing it." "If that is the case, I will take him with me," I replied.

Grizzly continued, "He is a Half Breed Negro, Yakky Indian. He comes from Mexico where he was wanted for many horrific massacres. It is told that he has been known to eat his victims. He is also wanted in America as well for the butchering of white settlers and Indians. They call him 'the Cannibal'. Even the Indians fear him, saying he is the Devil himself. If you plan to go after him, you might want to leave your woman and son where they will be safe. If he gets hold of them, there is no telling what he will do to them before he kills them. It will be so horrible and beyond anything, you can imagine. He has a bad way of torturing women and then leaving them for dead."

I closed my eyes trying not to remember Tapping Bird, and what she must have had to endure before she mercifully died. "I already know and that is why I am going to kill him. He killed my daughter and burned the house around her. He and his companions left my son, Toad, for dead and I promised Toad he would get his revenge. I am also sure if I even suggested that Running Water was to stay behind she probably would cut my heart out as I slept."

"Well then you had better get yourself a small army to go after him," Grizzly said. "He has evaded the Mexican and the American armies. I can see you already have a strong determined army and now you have one more. Let me get my gear and lets go kill us a monster," pausing between each word. He grabbed his gear and followed me out the door.

I knew I would need help if I were too encounter Cannibal. Although Toad was good with the Bow, he was still just a boy and no equal to this monster we were after. They would have to make every shot count because they would only get one chance. I was sure of that. We would have to kill him with our first shot. There was no certainty if he would be alone when we encountered him. Chances were he would be hiding behind a gang of ruthless killers just like himself.

We had enough supplies to last us for a couple of weeks if we rationed them and Grizzly had his own supplies. We also had to make sure we did not over exert the horses. They would need all their strength to ride and carry the loads across some of the most trying terrain in these mountains. We now had two pack animals, with the mule. Candy was not the most stable horse but she could carry a good size load.

The trail was leading us into the Northern Canadian Rocky Mountains towards the Yukon Territory. We trapped mink, beaver, shoot a couple of deer, and one Moose. Toad and Running Water would skin them and we would trade the hides to every trading post we came to.

Each time we would ask about the half-breed, if he had been there and if he had a gang with him. We knew we were on the right trail and getting close because they would tell us, "Yes, they had been hearing stories about him and his gang of killers." The trappers and prospectors along the rivers had been posting guards at their claims. They told of the two trappers that had been killed, butchered and eaten by these monsters.

They were not hunting for game; they would just raid the camps and take what they had. Although they did not come into the trading post, they had been spotted close by. The territory was in a state of fear for their families and they never ventured out alone to check their traps. There were always one or two men with them at all times, carrying a rifle that was cocked and ready to shoot. You never walked into a camp without first making sure they knew you, so be sure to yell.

Cannibal had a small army with him. I do not know what those men with a rifles cocked would be against those odds. We stopped at one of the trading posts and when we asked about Cannibal, the people inside just stopped talking. Then one of the trappers stepped up to me and said, "I guess you haven't heard about the boy who was taken from one of the trading posts up river. As Grizzly and I exchanged looks we said, "We haven't heard anything about a boy." He continued, "A couple of weeks ago a lone dark skinned half breed, mean looking savage went inside. He had a gun and pointed it at the trader telling him to give him all the shells on the shelf. He demanded a couple of the rifles as well. Then he shot and killed the clerk, dragging the boy outside knocking him unconscious and threw him on the back of his horse and rode away."

"A couple days' later two trappers came upon a recent camp where they found a dead fire pit and some bones that looked like they could have been the boy's. It was surmised he had been the evening meal for the gang. Fear has pretty much gripped this entire area, and quite a few of the trappers and their families have packed up and left. They figure there wasn't any fur that is worth losing their families for."

"The Northwest mounted Police from British Columbia have been tracking this gang, but they have been pretty crafty and have managed to elude even them. They have managed to be just one step ahead at every turn."

My small army of four continued to relentlessly follow their trail and vowed to kill each and every one of them. Their trail was not hard to follow. All we had to do was follow the bloody or burned bodies they left behind.

As we continued to ride high into the Canadian Rockies and cross the Continental Divide, our trail became more treacherous and narrow. So many times, there was not even an animal trail to follow. Some of the canyon walls cut by the centuries loomed high above our heads on one side and the cliffs where the river appeared to be just small winding snakes kept us in fear that if one of us made a misstep we would fall a thousand feet to our certain death.

Most times, we would lead our horses and the pack animals through the paths made by the mountain sheep. As the summer turned into fall, we knew we would have to find shelter before the winter over took us. We would have to halt our quest for the winter, but we would take it up again in the spring as soon as the snow would allow us. At the altitude of 16,000 feet, the air was very thin. We found it hard to breathe and with the horses carrying their heavy loads, they were struggling as well to keep up our pace and would tire easier.

The descent from the summit was much harder than the climb. The snow on the top had made the trail slippery and we had to be much more cautious. Jake, was in the lead, watching his footing and kept his pace slow, but Candy would be looking all around and not watching where she was walking. She was carrying most of the furs. Then there was the reliable Buddy that Running Water would ride with some of the furs and most of our food. Toad had developed a real attachment to Muley and preferred to ride him with some more of our supplies on his stout back and his surefooted walk. He was always careful where he put his feet. Grizzly would follow a short distance behind with his gelding and a mule loaded with more furs and supplies.

As we rounded a tight, steep corner, I could feel Jake slip. I stopped him and was just beginning to dismount when Candy, in her star gazing mode, ran into the rear of Jake. Before I could put my foot on the ground, Jake jumped to the side. About that time, Candy woke up and jerked the lead rope, leaving me off balance causing me to fall off the ledge. I was grabbing for anything I could, finally catching hold of a branch that was hanging out from a crevice in the rocks to stop my fall. However, by now, Candy was in a panic and was throwing her head, trying to lose the lead rope that was tied to my saddle horn. Jake kept his head and did not move to fight her crazy panic. When she was able to finally break lose, she was kicking rocks over the edge missing me by inches as I hugged the cliff wall. She was moving closer to the ledge, as she wrestled with the ropes.

Running Water had been watching as I fell over the edge. She had jumped to the ground and was trying to calm Candy, reaching for the rope. Before she could get it, Candy had gotten too close and lost her footing falling off the edge, so close, just missing me by inches. I could feel her body as she swept past me, falling to her death. Candy took with her all our furs and supplies. I could hear Running Water scream my name as she peered over the edge.

By now, Grizzly had handed his reins to Toad to hold as he ran to see where I was. He was certain I had met with my death, also.

His relief could be heard in his voice as he saw me just hanging on to my branch. He yelled down, "Hold on." He quickly ran to Jake, and grabbing the lariat, he wrapped it around the horn and came back, throwing the other end to me, again yelling, "Grab it and hold on tight." Then he told Running Water to go to Jake and lead him. I grabbed the rope, afraid I would not be strong enough. At first, I was afraid to let go of my branch, but I knew I had to so I leaped for it. Luckily, I was able to grab it and I held on for dear life as I was pulled to safety.

I collapsed on the ground weak from shaking. Finally, I was able to get my wobbly legs under me. Running Water was crying as she help to steady me. I reached for Jake, wrapping my arms around his neck pressing my face against his smooth thick neck. I could feel the low rumble coming from his throat, as he tried to comfort me, as if to say, "That's my job."

"Thank you for being the fantastic horse that you are. You never lost your senses during the entire ordeal. We could all three be at the bottom of this cliff if it was not for you. That poor dumb Candy," was all I could say. No one cared about all the furs and supplies we lost. It did not seem important. I held Running Water tight in my arms to calm her shaking and mine as well. Grizzly touched my shoulder shaking his head, "Someone up there was looking out for you today my friend." I glanced towards the Heavens saying a prayer of thanks.

As we led our horses the rest of the way through the narrow trail to a flat wide area. We thought it would be best for us to stop for the night and take an inventory of what we had lost. We talked about what we were going to do for the winter. It was coming on fast and the temperatures were dropping below freezing. We knew we had to get off the mountain, that was for sure. I was still upset about my near death experience and I couldn't get my hands to stop shaking, when Grizzly handed me a cup of hot coffee I spilled half of it before I could drink it. As we sat near the warm fire, I said, "You know I have never been so close to dying as I was today and it didn't feel good at all. I will be glad to get off these Mountains. I grew up in the Rocky Mountains of Colorado and I was never afraid. However, these Canadian Mountains have that evil feeling about them. I had a bad feeling from the time we started up them. They aren't like the mountains of my childhood."

"These feel sinister as if they are reaching out to you without any remorse. They have no spirit, no soul and no conscience. It will kill anyone that comes too close to the treasures it hides. It is a killer." Grizzly nodded, and said, "Once when I was a sailor we were sailing off the tip of Africa, I had the same feelings you are having. One day the sea would be calm and in the next instant, the wind would blow. The huge swells would crash against the side of the ship."

"It felt like it would swallow us up as they rose higher than the mast on the boat. It would never be the same from one day to the next. We never knew what to expect and we could not let our guard down. The feel of death was all around us."

"All I wanted was to get off the tip of Africa to a sea we knew. This one had an evil spirit that controlled its waters. I agree with you about this Mountain having an evil spirit and I for one cannot get out of here fast enough. This mountain wants to claim a soul and I believe it will claim many before this winter is finished. We have come close to losing one this day, notwithstanding our poor Candy."

We were all up before the sun was in the sky and after

eating a small breakfast, we packed and saddled our horses and were back on the trail just as the sun was peeking through the trees. We did not stop until we were on the valley below continuing to follow the river, crossing the portage to the Pelly River where we made camp for the night. We were all feeling a relief as we hobbled our horses and let them graze from the tall sweet grass. I could not help but to look back at the mountain that was almost my grave, saying another prayer, "Thank You."

We decided to stay here for a couple of days and set out traps to see if we could trap some Mink and Beaver. We needed to restock the supply that we had lost, and Grizzly had wanted to try his luck at gold panning from the river this morning, while Toad and I set the traps. We would need to put up a grubstake when we went into Dawson City.

Grizzly walked up river, about 30 yards just below the falls, which led into the river. There were narrows where the water was shallow and had slowed down. We thought that would be a good place to start. Grizzly's day was beginning to be a good one as he smiled and looked around at the vista that surrounded him. He thought to himself, "this is good and everything is good with the world today." He spent the next few hours just scooping the sand from the river bottom and checking to see if there was any color. It did not really matter to him if he found any or not. He decided to take a scoop close to a large rock in the middle of the river. He took a big scoop and started to swirl it around in his pan. Then he thought he saw something different about the rocks. He put his finger on it and moved his face closer to see what it was. He stumbled back almost dropping the pan before he regained his footing.

Gold, it was gold, a nugget the size of a Pearl. Then Grizzly began to move the sand around some more and then he saw it. The biggest nugget he had ever seen. It was the size of a Robin's egg and pure as anything he had ever imagined. He let out a war hoop that could be heard a mile away, and then he saw Aully and Toad.

Waving his arms and jumping up and down yelling for them to come on the run. They thought he was in trouble. They came running, slipping on the rocks almost falling in the river, before they reached him. He was yelling, "We're rich, we're rich" and grabbing Toad and Aully, lifting them off the ground he swung them both around in a circle. "We're rich, look what I found!"

Then he opened his fist and showed them his nugget. "Where did you find that?" Aully asked as they gaped at it in disbelief. Grizzly tried to explain he was just sticking his pan in the water and this is what he found.

Gold

"I am sure this spot is rich with nuggets, just like this one. We will have to keep this a secret until we can go to Dawson to stake our claim." "Whoa, wait now." I suddenly realized just what was going on here. "I have never done this before, and hadn't thought about prospecting. I was going to be a trapper and do not even know what to do. Will we have to tell anyone where our claim is? Won't that bring other prospectors here? Shouldn't we do some more panning just to be sure we have a claim?" Grizzly thought about that for a few minutes and then he said, "Yah, you might be right about that. We will stay here for a while, check this out, and do some more panning to be sure. We can never tell anyone where our claim is. We will wait a little longer. In the mean time, we will just continue as if we were trapping for Beaver and Mink, I said. "Toad and I will continue to trap and if anyone comes this way and asks questions, we will just say that we have trapped a few Beavers and Mink. Then when we go to Dawson, it will look like we are trading in our furs. That will give us a chance to do some investigating about staking a claim for our gold. What do you think about that?" "Yah," he said. "That is a good plan. Tomorrow you will trap and I will dig."

For the next week, we kept up our charade. When a couple of trappers wandered into our camp asking if we had any luck, I just held up a couple of furs and told them we had a few

Beaver, Mink and even got one Muskrat. We tried to do some gold panning but did not get any color. We figured there was more money in the trapping than in any gold we would find." So they just kept moving on down the river. In the meantime, Grizzly was having good sign and he already had a bag full of good size nuggets. He said he was a bit worried about the amount we already had and how were we going to cash it all in without causing a panic when we stake our claim. Besides, we did not know how to stake a claim and how much anonymity there would be.

Being unknowledgeable when we went to Dawson, we decided to make up some phony lie. We told the claim office we were planning to build a cabin along the river to spend the winter and thought we would do a little gold panning as well as trap. Figuring we would place a claim in case, we did find a little gold. The people in the office just laughed at us, thinking we were a couple of real Cheechako's (green horns). No one took us very seriously.

It was a known fact that anyone who had not lived in the wilderness for more than 9 to 12 months knew too little about surviving in the wilderness. Cheechako was the name the Indians called them. They would have to live here and grown a full face of whiskers promoting them to the noble name of Sourdough.

We split the nuggets and going separately cashed in small amounts at a time whenever we would bring in our furs to trade for supplies. We continued to do this for the rest of the winter and no one was the wiser, but as the winter began to ebb and spring thaws came, we realized we had a real dilemma to deal with. The claim was a big claim and we had accumulated quite a large cache of nuggets. Soon they would have to be cashed in. We talked it over and decided to take a chance and go to the essay office together, only cashing in half the nuggets.

As we walked up the steps to the front door of the office, we noticed a couple of suspicious characters loitering nearby, watching the comings and goings of prospectors with gold bags to cash in.

We had no choice. We had to cash in some of those nuggets. When the clerk dumped our bags of nuggets onto the weigh scale, he looked with wide-open eyes. He asked, "Where did you get these?" We did not say a thing at first. Then Grizzly asked in his gruff voice, "What are they worth?" He replied, "From what I can see you have about $2,000.00 worth of nuggets, but I will have to weigh them before I can give you a true value." We were speechless. "You fellows have a claim near here?" He asked. "When will you have these weighed?" I asked. He said. "Give me a few minutes." "We will wait." Grizzly and I stepped away and both said at the same time, "We need to find ourselves a good honest lawyer. We need to get some answers about how to protect our claim."

There was always the possibility we might have to use firepower to do that and no one wanted it to come to that. For now, we would wait until we had the money. We had done enough research to know the going rate at the time per ounce was $17.50. The total weight was 114.28 ounces and it came to exactly $2,000.00. We had to find a place to put it for safekeeping, before we left Dawson. We would not dare take it out of town after the news gets out we had it, for sure and for certain.

As we left the essay office, knowing the clerk could hardly

wait to tell someone about our gold nuggets we walked together down the street. I held my Winchester in one hand
ready for anything, leading Jake close behind me. We did not
like the way those seedy loiterers were watching us. We saw
a sign that said Attorney-at-Law hanging over the door just
down the street from the essay office, so we walked in. Grizzly
stepped up to the desk, asking to see the lawyer. The secretary
said he would be with them in a moment that he was with a
client, smiling a weak shy smile. Grizzly told her we would
wait and sat down on a chair that looked too small for his huge
body.

After an hour had past, Grizzly had about enough of that
little uncomfortable chair. He just got up and walked to the
lawyer's office door. The secretary tried to stop him by stepping in front of him, saying, "No, no, you can't go in there."
Grizzly took her by both shoulders and sat her back down at
her desk and said, "No one should have so many problems that
it would take an hour to solve" and then he turned and walked
to the door and opened it. I could not see what he saw but by
his reaction, I knew it must be something special.

Grizzly had stopped in his tracks and stepped back.
Laughing in his loud voice he said, "I guess maybe I was mis-
taken. This is not something anyone should rush through." I
stepped up next to him looking into the room. Together we
just stood there laughing our heads off. The attorney was with
a woman of the night in a very compromising position as he had
her bent over his desk, naked from the waist down, her skirt
thrown over her head. His pants were down to his ankles. On
the floor was an empty bottle of whiskey. It was obvious what
was happening here. "Excuse me; proceed with what you are

doing. Our business is not that important." Laughing Grizzly turned and walked out the door. I followed behind hardly able to breathe I was laughing so hard. Back on the street Grizzly said, "I guess I have been in the wilderness for too long and forgot the rules of talking to a lawyer." I could not help but add my two cents. "I wonder if that is the going fee for an hour with an attorney." We both laughed at that.

In the meantime, the attorney was scrambling to get his pants up and fastened as he ran out into the lobby. The red-faced painted girl was giggling, tugging, and pulling her skirt down as she ran out the back door of his office. Grizzly turned to me and said, "I think we will handle this in our own way from now on." The lawyer came running out the door after pointing his finger at his secretary and yelling, "You're fired!" He continued until he was in the street, shaking his fist and yelling, "Don't you bother to come back either." I just looked back at him and laughed as I followed Grizzly down the street. "Can't afford your fees," I yelled back.

We finally went to the claims office and upon entering; we asked if they knew of anyone who can keep their pants on that, we could talk to about a gold claim. The man there laughed and said, "It seems you have already met our esteemed local lawyer Mister Jeremiah Pike." He told us to come on into his office and sit down. He thought that maybe he could help us.

After a slight hesitation, we followed him and sat down. "Now what can I do for you?" he asked as he sat behind a huge dark polished Mahogany desk. "We would like to place a claim, but we don't know how to go about it." We said in unison. The big man laughed and then he said, "I assume that was your purpose for going to see Mr. Pike." "Yes it was. We just don't want to be cheated by some shark," Grizzly answered looking suspiciously at the man. The man grinned and then he continued, "I don't blame you. There are a lot of those Sharks out there.

"Well, there is such a thing as a Placer Claim, but one or both of you would have to give the exact location or a close proximity location as well as a precise description of it. Then you will have to have a signed witness that will verify your statement is factual as to where your claim is located. Then it would have to be registered with the claim office, but that would not be entirely necessary. I wouldn't worry about it unless it is a substantial producing claim."

Nevertheless, after he looked at us and surmised we were sitting on a good deposit, he said, "Then you had best show a registered claim or anyone could say it was theirs and you had claim jumped it from them."

"Most miners would respect that it was yours, but there are those who sit at the land office watching for the novice to walk out and not have a registration, like Lawyer Pike who has his Goons watch for him. I would not trust that man as far as I could spit; he likes to word his documents to suit himself, with his creative fine print and before they know it the miners have lost their claims."

Both Grizzly and I indicated that no one was going to steal our claim. "Then I assume you have a substantial claim," he continued. We did not say yea or nay to that remark. He stopped talking for a moment, leaned back in his chair, and looked us over as he peered from over his glasses and said, "First of all, I want you both to know I am not your enemy. I already have enough gold of my own to buy half the claims in the Canadian Territory two times over. I do not need yours. I am here only to make sure the sleazy thieves and cutthroats that just prey on the unsuspecting families do not cheat the hard working miners who have come a long way to prospect for gold. I am also not a lawyer, but I made sure I was educated and I do know the laws pertaining to the gold claims. I also know a lot about investing money matters."

"I like the two of you and I believe you are smart, but you are out of your element when it comes to these types of things. I don't blame you for not trusting anyone, as well you shouldn't." He talked a bit longer and told us about himself. He said his name was Jackson Cord. When I said my name was Aully Samuel Lawson, that I came from the Lawson Homestead on the Grand Mesa in Colorado, he stared at me as if he had seen a ghost. Almost in a whisper, he asked as he put his hand over his chest. "Your Mamma and Daddy, aren't by chance John and Ingabar Lawson are they?" "Yes they are," was my reply. "I'm sorry to seem so speechless, but I am "The" Jack Cord, the Wagon Master that brought those two very young, innocent, but determined kids in the wagon train to Colorado."

For the rest of the day we talked and exchanged stories about the ranch, while Grizzly listened and laughed at the stories. Jack was to become our best confidant, adviser mentor and most of all, our best friend. We became deeply indebted to his sound words. He advised us on how to protect ourselves against the no good that was always lurking at the essay office just waiting for their next prey. He had his main office in Fort Selkin.

Before we left heading back to the cabin to tell Running Water and Toad all about our meeting with Jack, we had put our money in the bank owned by Jack, keeping just enough to buy the supplies we would need for the next few months.

He advised us to write up some kind of agreement between us in the chance that something would happen to one of us. This was to assure the survivor would then become the sole owner of the claim. He called it a personal will. We went back to our hotel room and immediately spent the day sitting at the little table in our room making out our wills. Then we tried to figure out how much money we would need to survive for the next month and how much we should leave in the Bank of Jack Cord.

It was late when we realized we had not eaten. We were thinking maybe we should try to find a good place to get some grub, when there was a knock at the door. We looked at each other and grabbed for our pistols. Grizzly stepped behind the door as I gruffly yelled, "Who is it and what do you want?" A soft voice answered, "Mister Cord would like for you to join him in the dining room for supper." I opened the door to find a small blonde haired, very well dressed little boy of about 10 years old standing there very sheepishly. He smiled and said, "My Daddy wants you to meet his family and he wants us to meet you."

It had been over a week since Aully and Grizzly had left for Dawson City. Running Water was becoming very uneasy. Toad said that maybe he should ride into Dawson to see if they were still there. "Maybe, they had run into some bandits or the renegade Indians that have been roaming the territory." Running Water said she was afraid to be alone here after what happened to Tapping Bird and what they had been hearing about the Cannibal gang of killers.

She was stretching a hide over a wide plank when she

looked up to see two riders coming into camp. They did not look like prospectors, but they did a lot of looking around at everything before they asked, "Where are your men?" Running Water could feel the chills run up her back as fear began to set in. She told them, "The Men," emphasizing the word "Men" "were just down the river a ways and would be back in just a few minutes."

The fat man laughed and said, "I don't think so. I think you are here alone and maybe you need a lesson about what happens to a lying Indian squaw." Just as he was starting to dismount from his horse a shot rang out hitting the dirt at his horse's hind feet, making the horse jump. Before the rider could regain his balance, he fell with a hard thud to the ground. A deep voice was heard to say, "And maybe not. I think you had better Git! As Toad stepped out from around the corner of the cabin with the Winchester aimed in their direction. The second man reached for his rifle, but before he could get it out of its scabbard, Toad had aimed and pulled the trigger, hitting the man in the shoulder. Once more, he yelled, "I said Git! Or my next shot will find a spot right between your eyes."

The fat one was picking himself up and trying to get on his spooked horse, while the injured man was grabbing his shoulder trying to stop the bleeding, whining, "You little bastard, you shot me." By now Running Water had retrieved one of the pistols saying as she stepped closer to the fat man, "Don't ever underestimate what an Indian squaw and a young man can do when they are threatened. Now "Git" and don't come back this way again or I promise there will be no talking." They turned and galloped into the forest from the direction they had come. Toad asked without taking his eyes off the direction the two men had gone, "Do you think they will be back?" Running Water looked at her son proudly and answered, "I don't know, but I do know for sure if it was me, I wouldn't, after the ass kicking they just got from a tough guy like you." She smiled, turning towards the trail into town where Aully and Grizzly had gone. Toad slowly started to grin and nodded his head. "Darn right!" he said to himself.

As we neared the cabin we were laughing and joking about how we were going to tell Running Water and Toad about Jack Cord and all our news, when we heard the sound of a rifle coming from up river. Fear gripped me when I heard the second shot. I spurred Jake, with Buddy coming behind loaded down with all the supplies. This sound was all too familiar as pictures of Tapping Bird flashed before me.

When I saw Running Bird standing there I reined in my stallion and jumped off before he stopped, running to her and pulled her into my arms. Then I saw Toad standing there tall with the rifle in his hand. He was wearing a slight smile on his face, flushed with excitement as if he had a secret he just could not wait to tell me. Everyone started talking at the same time, as there was so much to tell each other of what had happened here. Worried I looked all around and then looked at Grizzly he also looked worried.

We put it aside for the moment and began to tell about our trip to Dawson. We spent the evening talking and laughing about the last couple of days and all that had been accomplished. I wanted to have Jack meet Running Water and Toad.

Next day Grizzly took Toad aside putting his huge arm around his shoulders saying, "You are no longer a boy. You are a man and you will never be called Little Toad again. From now on, you will be known as Toad the Warrior and you will hold your head high. I am very proud of you and how you protected your mother." Then he slapped him on the back and walked away. Toad stood there stunned for just a moment. Then he smiled and with his chin out, he held his head high and said, "Yes, I am a warrior today and from this day forward I will walk proud."

We worked hard to build a stockpile of furs and gold nuggets, but some of the seedy characters in town were noticing even though we tried to conceal our cache of nuggets. We always made sure to take a different route back to the cabin. Eventually we could not hide our wealth, even though we never carried any of the money on us. We took Jack's advice and deposited it all in the bank. Trying not to spend it on luxury things only the staples we needed. Word was beginning to spread that there had been a rich gold strike on the river. The location and which river we never disclosed. We only had just so many routes we could take without being discovered, on the Yukon River.

By 1890 after the discovery of gold in California, there was a rush of people bringing hundreds for the dream of wealth. By 1896-1897, word had reached all the way to New York and Europe. Then word got out of the gold in Canada and Alaska. People were told the gold nuggets were just lying on top of the ground and that all they had to do was to pick them up and put them in a basket. No one told them of the horrible hardships they would have to face just to be in this forbidden land to get to the gold fields.

They came in hordes bringing their families and children with few belongings. They had no knowledge of the harsh cold winds and snow that at times the only thing you could see for miles was ice, in addition, to the blinding white snow. The mountain trails lead straight up and for miles, all you could see was a snake line of men and women, some carrying huge backpacks. Some were crawling just to get through the deep path to the top.

Word soon got out about the avalanche on Chilkoot Pass that buried 100 people, horses, and sleds loaded with supplies. The "Chinook" would come almost overnight and melt the snow so rapidly, turning it to freezing water, bringing with it floods and mudslides burying bodies of the unsuspecting prospectors. There were many avalanches ending dreams of striking it rich.

Crude rafts were built in haste to carry all their supplies down river where the Taiya River and the Skagway River merged north into Lake Bennet. The canyon narrowed there creating swift rapids where huge boulders bulged out of the water causing more strong dangerous currents as the water flowed down the canyon. The Indians would refer to them as Lotsa Skootum Water. Only one in ten ever made it through before they capsizing losing their lives and everything they had. Many men, women, children, and animals would die in these waters.

The Indians let it be known, they would carry all their supplies over the passes for a large amount of money. Some of the prospectors figured it would be better to pay the price than to lose everything they had. Losing their gear left very little chance that they would be able to recoup. Some just gave up and headed back to civilization. They had already suffered enough.

Many still came with determination bringing with them everything from horses, which did not do to well in the deep snow and cold, to dogs, used to pull sleds. They brought goats for milk, but mostly they were butchered for food, which was a commodity then, as food was scarce. The most valuable commodity were the oxen they brought. They could withstand the weather and the terrain. Once they had reached their destination, the oxen were sold to the hordes of men who came, paying top dollar for them. Steak was the most important food on the menu. It could also be made into jerky for the trail.

The price of food at the trading post was exorbitant. One potato would cost as much as $10.00. After the word got out about our gold strike, it was hard to do any panning of our own. It did not take long before there were miners who came building their sluice slide just down river.

They even built them just above us on the river. Although they made sure, they did not infringe on our claim it was not long until the gold ran out.

Many times we had to use force to keep a few of them from coming into our claim area and we would take turns standing guard 24 hours a day.

Grizzly and I would make a trip to trade in our gold and furs. On one of those particular trips, after we had finished our business we decided to go to the saloon and have a drink. As we walked into the crowded room, the smell of smoke and the stench of the miners' sweaty bodies were almost more then we could take, and we almost turned to leave. Then Grizzly heard one of the miners at the bar say something to another man, who was leaning up against the bar with his foot resting on the foot railing.

"Did you hear about the massacre up on the 40 Mile River?" Grizzly stepped to the bar to listen. "There was a camp where five men were building a sluice when suddenly a gang of men came out of nowhere shooting them all in a surprise attack before they could even get to their guns. Two days later a couple of trappers found them. Two of them had been eaten, leaving the others for dead. One of the miners was just barely alive when they found them. He was able to tell about it before he died." Everyone in the bar stopped to listen. Grizzly stepped closer and asked, "Are you sure they had been eaten by those same men or was it animals who ate them?" "No, no" was the reply. "It was those men because they took the time to roast the meat over an open pit and the bones were identified as human.

A chill ran through me as Grizzly told me what he heard. We had been so busy with our mining claim I had just about forgotten about the monster they called Cannibal and his gang of killers. "What were they doing so far north and what was he doing on the 40 Mile River?" Grizzly and I looked at each other with the same

Thought. We had to get back to our cabin, and get ourselves and the other miners near us prepared for what might happen if Cannibal decided to come up the Yukon River, where we were. We rode as fast as we could. We had to warn Running Water and Toad and plan our strategy with our neighbors. We decide that one of us would always be guarding the camp, either Grizzly or Myself.

After two weeks, there had been no incident so Grizzly left to go to the fort with Toad to get the supplies we had forgotten in our haste to get back to camp.

Next day three men rode into our camp. One of the men was a short stout man with a thin scraggily beard. The other one, on a painted pony, was an Indian wearing the black vest of the buffalo. I was not so concerned about them, but the one who stayed back at a short distance was the one who caught my attention.

He was a huge, ugly, black, half breed with a fierce looking face full of hate with heavy dark eyebrows. A deep scar was visible under the dirty tobacco spattered, beard which stretched from the side of his mouth to his ear. Instantly I recognized him from the description Toad had told about the man who attacked Tapping Bird.

I told Running Water to stay inside with the Winchester cocked and stay out of sight but to be sure to aim it at the black man in the rear. Be sure you kill him first if they do anything. I did not want them to see her. I had my 44 revolver in my hand cocked and I made sure they saw it as I crossed my hand over my other one in front of me. They rode up to me within 30 feet before I spoke, "That's close enough. State your business." They stopped and said, "We mean no trouble. We were just wondering if you might have some grub you would be able to spare. We haven't had anything to eat for a couple of days." "No" I replied, "We have just enough for ourselves." The ugly one looked all around nudging his horse forward and then he said, "Who else is here? I do not see anyone. Where is the rest of your household?"

Just about that time a shot rang out as Running Water stepped from the doorway, cocking the Winchester again as she did, "Does that answer your black ass question?" About the same time, two miners from up river came out into the clearing with their rifles aimed at the men on their horses. "Thought you were having a party, Aully, and thought we would join you." "Weren't no party, these men were just leaving," I said, not taking my eyes off the three men. The three men looked us over for just a moment then they turned their horses, yelling back as they rode out of camp, "Not very hospitable of you."

No one lowered their rifles until they were sure they had left and were gone. "Who the hell were they? We saw them heading for your camp and from the looks of them we knew they meant no good. Figured you might need some help, after you told us about the massacre up on the 40 Mile River."

Running Water came running up to my side when she heard that. She was still gripping tight to the cocked Winchester. "What massacre are they talking about up 40 Mile River? She asked. "Was he the monster that killed my Tapping Bird? Were they the ones?" If I had known, I would have killed him today." "Yes, I know you would have, but I am not sure. "Most likely he is the one." Then I looked at the two miners and said, "If they are the ones I think they are, they have moved onto the Yukon River territory and we have to get together and make a plan to protect ourselves. We need to put together some semblance of law. These men are vicious killers and they kill just for the fun of it. If you have any family with you, make sure you have plenty of protection for them and be sure they know how to shoot a gun."

The miners left on a run to get back to their camps, yelling they would spread the warning all up and down the river and we would meet back here in two days to make a plan. That night we slept holding each other and remembering. I made a vow that I would never let anything happen to the love of my life, Running Water. There was no sleeping for me that night as I listened for any sound out of the ordinary that would alert me to danger, but by morning, I surrendered to sleep and was startled awake. "It's alright my love. I have the rifle here next to me and I will keep it here while I make you some coffee and fix breakfast for you." She was trying to hide her fear, but I knew her too well and it could not be hidden.

Grizzly and Toad came back from the fort late the next day with some bad news from up the Stewart River. They described a horrible scene they had heard from Jack Cord. All along the river on their crude rafts, miners were lined up trying to get to the gold fields.

Some of the miners were smart and hired the Indians to pack their gear over the mountain. There were a few who either did not have the money or did not want to part with what they had, thinking the Indians were trying to just rip them off and steal their gear. Those miners decided to run the rapids thinking it could not be as bad as they say.

Once they started, there was no turning back. They overloaded their crude rafts and there was no way to control them on the rapids. When the rafts overturned, they were so worried about saving their gear that they forgot to save themselves. At the headwaters, gear and broken mangled bodies began to emerge. They counted 85 bodies. Only 1 in 10 made it and he was in bad shape, just hanging onto a log.

The melting snow had made the rapids impassable, but they had been warned. We listened to this story in horror thinking, "What price for gold?" It only made men careless and stupid to risk everything they had for it.

When Grizzly stopped talking he looked down at his feet then almost in a whisper he began again, "Aully that is not the worst of it. Maybe Running Water needs not hear this. It is pretty awful as it involves "Cannibal." She stepped forward and said, "Don't think for one minute I am leaving." "I was afraid of that," he said almost to himself. "Cannibal" has built himself quite a large gang of killers. They have no boundaries as to what horror they will inflict on these poor, dumb, money hungry, fools.

He and his gang have attacked and massacred three mining claims along the 40 Mile River. They killed everyone but the children, which they carried off when they left. They are being used to feed the gang. Evidence showed there was a large fire pit where the remaining bones of small children were found. "Aully, these are the worst Monsters that I have ever heard of."

"The Canadian Mounted Police are soliciting for more men to join their posse to go after the Cannibal Gang of killers. There has been a reward posted so vigilante men from all over are coming to join up, even some from America. Many of the men who are joining up are nothing more than killers themselves. I fear they will become a vigilante band of killers themselves and no one will be able to tell the good guys from the bad ones."

I told him about the three men who came into the camp and figured them to be some of the sign-ups, but the big ugly one was most definitely "Cannibal" himself. Maybe the other two were some that he was recruiting for his gang. A chill ran through me. This could be a very ugly time for all the miners and families. I had thought about maybe we should leave here for our own good and for the safety of my own family.

How bad this was going to be remained to be seen, but people were beginning to fear for their lives. What were the intentions of this gang and how far were they willing to go? Obviously pretty far to be doing the things they are doing. I felt a deep uneasiness and fear. There were only four of us. How could we protect our own camp?

I knew I had to warn the others of just how dangerous this was getting and soon Cannibal would run out of camps on the 40 Mile River. Then where would he go? "Would he come up the Yukon River?" It looked like to me he was already scouting us out and it would not be long until we were also on his list to raid.

We had to get everyone along the river to create a group of our own to protect what was ours, without causing a panic and worse, a vigilante gang of our own. The panic could cause someone to kill one of our own by mistake. Word was sent to all the camps to gather at the Grizzly-Aully camp in two hours.

Grizzly told everyone what he had heard on his trip to the fort. They talked long into the night with lots of shouting and threats about how they would kill those bastards and how they would deal with them if they ever tried to come into their camp, but in the end, they all knew they could not protect themselves unless they got organized and had a plan.

Grizzly proposed that they take turns and created security guards to patrol the river at all times. Maybe wear a colored scarf to identify them, so no one would shoot them by mistake. If someone we did not know came up river fire a volley of two shots to alert everyone. That is what they decided to do. The first groups of three were decided upon to patrol for the first

6 hours then another group of six took over. The woman from each camp made a colored scarf for the men of their camp, to be worn on their hats.

For the next week, all was quiet. The tension was unbearable and everyone was jumpy. About the beginning of the next week a volley of two shots rang out, pause, then another volley of two. Everyone ran for his or her rifles and everyone was ready for whatever was coming up the river. Two men in uniforms came into our camp and identified themselves as Royal Canadian Mounted Police; they said they were checking to see if we had seen anyone suspicious. I had never seen a mounted police officer before and they were very impressive to look at. They had on red jackets and blue pants. Mostly I was aware of their look of confidence as they sat on their tall, long-legged horses. They were formal looking, but it was obvious they knew what they were about.

I told them about the three men that rode into our camp and described them to the officers. The Captain then asked if anyone had any experience in law enforcement. They were recruiting men to go after the "Cannibal Gang. They needed volunteers. No one stepped forward. The miners said, "We came to Canada to hunt for gold not outlaws." Toad jumped up and said he wanted to join up; Running Water was shocked and protested very loudly. The officer asked him, "How old are you?" Toad replied, "I am old enough and I can shot a rifle as well as any man here and I am a marksman with the bow." The officer was almost going to say yes, until he looked at the face of the mother and said, "I'm sorry son. I know you are brave and you are good with the bow and the rifle, but we do not take anyone under the age of 18. Maybe in a year or two come see me again."

His head down, Toad turned and kicking the dirt as he walked away. I knew he was mad and humiliated, but I was relieved the officer refused his willingness. I went to him and said, "Toad you are the most valuable person here and I will need you to help keep your mother safe from harm. I cannot be here every minute. You have already shown how brave you are. I am afraid for her safety and I know you can protect her." "I would die before I would let any harm come to her," was his reply. I had hoped for this reply. I grabbed him by his shoulders, looked him in the eyes and said, "There is no one I would trust with that job. I love her very much and would not be able to live if anything happened to her."

It was the season of the 24 hours of daylight and the air was warm, with the river easing to a small trickle. Many of the miners had set up claims all along the Yukon River, but it was obvious the gold was playing out. Grizzly had become restless so when he came to me I knew he was thinking of moving on. He said, "We have a good size stake in the bank now, enough to do whatever we want with our futures. Almost as rich as Jack Cord." He smiled, "I don't believe there will be many more big nuggets found here. Maybe we should give our claim to one of these miners and move on into the Northern Alaskan Territory. We can head for the Tanana River and follow it to Fairbanks. There could be some good trapping and maybe some gold along the River. What do you think, Partner?" I was not surprised, as I saw the relief in his face when I said, "I think you are right. We are getting too crowded here."

That night we gingerly approached this idea to Running Water and Toad. Surprisingly they were both in agreement.

They were getting restless and thought heading into the wilderness again was a great idea.

The next day we signed our claim over to one of the miners, who had been there the longest. Gathering all our gear, we loaded our pack animals and rode out of the camp. We headed for Fort Selkin and the Jack Cord Bank to collect our money and buy supplies.

Our first stop was to say goodbye to Jack. He was not too glad to see us go, but he understood and wished us well. He also told us to be very careful, as the Cannibal Gang had been spotted along the Yukon River near Rampart, Alaska. I assured him we would keep a vigilant eye out for them. Our next stop was to the bank where we withdrew all our money and closed the account. Then we cashed in all our furs and gold. We divided all our money between the four of us; we didn't want to have just one of us carrying that much cash in one place, in the case that something would happen and we were separated.

Not Forgotten

It felt good to be on the trail again. Everyone was in a happy mood as we laughed, teasing each other about all that had happened to us and what we had done this last year. Grizzly was in the lead with his pack mule, Running Water was riding Buddy behind him, and leading another packhorse. Toad was on "Muley" and then myself, bringing up the rear with my faithful Jake, leading another packhorse. I looked at my friend, Grizzly, thinking, "What a fine man he was and how lucky to have him in my life."

There was a mystery about him. He spoke of being on a ship on the tip of Africa. I never asked about that and he never volunteered any information. He was much older than I was, but he never slacked on a job and he always listened to my ideas as if I really knew what I was talking about. I then looked at my beloved Running Water. My heart swelled with the love I felt for her. I could not imagine what my life would have been without her. I would have such a swelling in my chest every time I looked at her beautiful face. I never thought I could love someone so much. Then as I looked at my adopted son, Toad, I watched him as he rode Muley behind his mother, keeping her between him and Grizzly to protect her if he needed to. He sat tall in the saddle, straight-backed and watching in all directions for any sign of danger. I was so proud of him.

He had grown into a very handsome young man with his

long black hair below his shoulders, which he tied back with a leather strap to keep it from blowing in his eyes. He was tall and lean and the leather vest he wore fit snug around his muscled chest. He wore the beaded neckband Running Water had made for him with great pride. She had told him it was a sign to everyone that he was a Warrior.

Grizzly had given him a 44 revolver with a side holster, which he also wore around his waist. The belt was filled with the bullets for his Winchester Rifle that he bought at the post. He had the rifle snuggly strapped in the scabbard that hung on the side of his saddle. Every morning he would practice his shooting until he became an expert sharpshooter. I knew if I ever needed someone to protect my back I would never need anyone else but him. I was to find out soon just how valuable he would be.

That night we had not made much distance, but we decided to set up camp at the headwaters of the White River. Figuring we had another 100 miles to go before we got to Fairbanks, Alaska. We knew we had crossed the border into Alaska 20 miles back. The air was warm, but with the 24 hours of daylight, we had a hard time keeping track of the time we spent in the saddle. So at one of our stops we bought a clock. It was hard getting used to using it to tell the time of day. We had never needed one before. We were accustomed to getting up at daylight and going to bed at dark.

We knew we could not keep traveling for the sake of the horse's, if not for our own. The horses and pack animals needed to rest and graze from their heavy loads. We would travel a couple of days then we would take a couple of days off to give us time to recoup. During that time, Grizzly would pan for gold while Toad and I would do some trapping.

Running Water took to grooming and checking the animals for sores from the constant rubbing of the heavy packs. She would put salve on their sores from a remedy she had learned from her people. She loved walking among them, checking their hooves, combing their manes, and just talking to them. They would follow her around the meadows like little puppies.

Later, while we sat eating our meals we would sit around the fire and talk until we got tired. Then we would go to bed, letting our fatigue tell us when it was time. Running Water would be the first one to rise in the morning, she had a sense as to when it was time; and build a fire to fix the coffee and breakfast for everyone when we got up. After eating, we would round up the animals, repack everything, saddle our horses, and continue our journey.

After the fourth day of traveling, we started to feel that uneasy feeling as we approached the "Little 40 Mile River." No one felt like joking or kidding around so we rode in silence. I had seen signs of many horses in the mud along the Tanana River and at one point there had been a bed of old ashes in a pit where someone had fixed a meal. I rode up next to Grizzly and asked what he thought about it. Before he could answer Running Water, rode up saying the ashes were about a week old and there had been 10 or 12 riders. They had been carrying a light load and were moving in a hurry. She also said that half of them veered off and headed northwest while the rest were ahead of us following the river. I did not like the sound of that, as there could be an ambush waiting up ahead for us. I was sure it was the Cannibal Gang, but either way we had to continue heading for the fort and most likely at some point, we were going to encounter them.

At our next stop, we took an inventory of our ammunition and guns, making it a point to have them ready to use at a seconds notice. I asked Running Water which gun she would want to have and to my surprise she said, "The Winchester." I asked her, "Are you sure, do you know how to use it?" She replied, "Toad had been taking me out and showing me how to shoot it in quick order, by keeping it to my shoulder and cocking it after each shot, making sure I did not lose sight of my target." When I asked Toad about it, he told me she was a good shot with the rifle, and would practice whenever I went to the fort with the furs and gold. She said she was never going to be a victim.

We hurried along the river without any incidences. We wanted to get to the trading post as soon as we could. We did not want to camp outside tonight, alone. This small trading post was built just to accommodate the miners and trappers who stopped to fix their saws, axes, picks, and whatever else they needed done. All the other businesses had left when the gold had started to run out. Only the saloon with an old man bartender, a blacksmith and a small supply store remained. A couple of old tired miners ran the store figuring they would be able to take life easy in their old age.

Just as we rounded the bend in the river, we heard the sound of gunfire. It sounded like the Fort was were under siege. I yelled at Grizzly, that we had better tether the pack animals and go in prepared for a fight. We had no idea what we would be riding into or how many. I told Running Water and Toad to stay with the pack animals but they would hear nothing of it, saying they could do better to help the fort and I could not convince either to stay behind. There was no time to argue with them.

As we turned the bend in view of the post, we could see the saloon on fire. The black smoke billowed overhead and the old timer was lying face down in a pool of blood not moving. Two of the outlaws were also lying in the middle of the muddy road, dead. Horses were running loose, riderless. Rifle barrels were stuck out the small peepholes in the doors of the post, but to our horror the outlaws had surrounded the post and those inside were not going to make it out alive without help. Two of the outlaws had climbed on the roof and were trying to dislodge the chimney; using it to get inside. I pulled out my 44 pistol and fired a shot into the head of one of them causing him to tumble to the ground. By then Toad had shot the other one. Both of them hitting the ground at the same time, with a thud, in the mud.

It was then the leader saw us. He wore a bearskin coat, his collar hugging his face, black as coal. I could see in his eyes the hate and evil that raged from them. My first thought was, "Oh, my God it's the Devil himself." He spurred his horse and turning headed straight for me. Fear as I had never known gripped me as I shot once, going wild, I missed. Again, I fired hearing a thud, I thought it hit him, veering left he turned and appeared to head for the forest. I remember thinking "You Cowardly Bastard, leaving your men to fight your fight."

It was then that I felt Jake stumble. I realized the thud I heard was the bullet hitting him in the chest; he fell to the street with me trapped under his huge body. Dazed I could hear the shooting all around me. Grizzly rode like a lunatic into the middle of the gang hitting everyone he aimed at, leaving men lying on the muddy ground. Toad was riding low and aiming from under the neck of his mule. They looked like the warriors of old, leaving the outlaws confused and dazed. They did not know where we had come from. It was more than they had anticipated.

As I struggled to get out from under the heavy weight of Jake, I looked up to see the face of the black monster coming for me anticipating his last kill. Then the sound of a repeating Winchester filled the air, as I turned to see where it was coming from, I saw the face of Running Water. Her face filled with the rage and hate she had kept inside of her for so long. She was walking and firing the rifle aiming from the shoulder; each shot hitting its target. She would cock it and fire again until she had emptied the chamber into the chest of the man who had haunted her dreams. The monster known as, "The Cannibal," with a look of disbelief, fell to his death, face down in the mud like a pile of trash.

Then there was silence all around for what seemed like forever. I could hear the sound of a squeaky door as it was slowly opened and the storekeeper emerged gingerly looking all around. I looked to see where Running Water was and saw Toad dismount from his mule before it had time to stop and run for the body lying on the ground.

"Oh...no...no... Running Water what have you done?" I struggled to get free from my trap, crying, then Grizzly appeared from out of nowhere, grabbing the saddle horn and lifting Jake off my legs setting me free. I struggled to my feet and ran to my wife and son. Toad was holding her in his arms; tears running unashamed down his face.

He rocked her body, "Mamma...Mamma." He cried, telling her, "Hold on. Don't die. You will be alright." When he saw me he said, "I wasn't there when she needed me. I am sorry." I grabbed them in my arms and then he handed her to my waiting arms, gently telling her as he kissed her cheek, "I love you." As I cradled her in my arms holding her close to my chest, I asked her, "Why did you have to be so brave?" In a whispered voice she said, "I love you. I couldn't let him hurt you." Then she closed her eyes and relaxing against my chest, she let out a long sigh and she was gone. I cried, "I love you my sweet wife. I will always love you, my sweet Running Water," as I rocked her in my arms. I hadn't noticed Grizzly standing behind me as he placed his hand on my shoulder. I didn't see his tears.

In the days that followed, Grizzly and Trader built a scaffold for her and after wrapping her body in a Bear Skin blanket; they laid her body upon it. I could do nothing. I had no heart to continue our journey. I sat by her, not able to move or eat. Everything was gone. I had no heart or hope. All was gone. She had become my entire life. My sun, my moon, my stars, everything I did was for her and now that was gone. I must have cried a million tears. Toad would come and sit with me as we silently let our grief mingle, but nothing would help. Our loss was too great.

I knew people had come to the trading post after they heard about the battle. They would help with the burial of the old timer from the saloon. They even helped to dig a mass grave for the outlaws. Toad said he wanted to burn the monster, "Cannibal" but he was told it would not be humane. "Why?" He asked. "This was a monster that ate children. He killed and raped my sister and killed my mother. He had no honor and he is not entitled to any humane treatment. "He was the Devil." Grizzly said, "I agree, but we are men of honor."

I do not know how long I sat there, as I had lost all sense of time. All I could feel was my pain. Grizzly came and led me away. He sat me down and looking at me he said, "Aully, I loved her too. Everyone who had ever met her loved her, but we have to let her spirit go. She cannot go to the ancestors, as long as you hold her here. You have to let her go to her people."

I forced myself to eat realizing how hungry I was. I would eat like a starving man, but my stomach was weak and I would lose it. After a while, I started to eat with a little more control and was able to eat and drink again. Sometime later, I could not tell, as I had lost all sense of time, a troop of Mounted Police came into the post. They had heard about the killings.

They heard about Running Water and offered their condolences. Then they asked if any of the rest of the outlaws had escaped. I remembered the one that had ran for the forest and abandoned his men as he sneaked into the forest to hide. I thought it was the Cannibal.

I tried to remember what I had seen. A black man fitting the description of Cannibal did ride into the forest. Nevertheless, who was the black man that Running Water had shot and killed? Were there two of them that looked alike? I had to think about it. He could not have come back so soon. It did seem like he came back fast after I fell to the ground. The police said they had reason to believe this "Cannibal" was still on the move and has rejoined his gang and they were heading back into Canada. I tried to describe the man I saw. Kinky black hair, dark Indian skin. However, he had a beard and if he had a scar, I could not be sure. All I could really be sure of were those black evil eyes. The officer looked at me and said, "That sounds like the man we are after."

"I don't understand." I said. "We killed him and buried him in a mass grave with the rest of those killers." The constable looked at me for a moment then he said, "I am afraid you may have killed the wrong man. Some say he had a twin brother who looked exactly like him. That is why it has been so hard to catch him. He would be in one place and then two days later he would be 100 miles from there."

"You mean to tell me Running Water died thinking she had killed the killer of Tapping Bird?" "I'm sorry, but it looks like that." All this time Toad had been listening to our conversation. "Sir, if you are going after him I would like to volunteer to go with you." "No," I said. "I can't lose you, too." Grizzly put his hand on my shoulder and said, "He is no longer a boy, and we have to let him go his own way. We have taught him all we can. He will make a good policeman." I knew he was right. Between the two of us, we had taught him to read, write, add figures, and shoot, but most of all we had taught him to be just and honorable.

He would make a good Royal Mounted Policeman. He was a man, but he was also a warrior. I said many times that if I were ever in trouble, I would want him at my side knowing he would fight to the death to save me and he believes in honor and justice.

The Constable looked at him, "Haven't I seen you before? Aren't you the young man who wanted to go after the scar faced man with me a year or so ago?" "Yes, I was." Toad answered, "But I was a boy then. Today I am a man and a warrior."

The Constable looked intently at him and said, "I can see

that, and you have certainly proven yourself worthy from what others have said about you. But what does your father think about you becoming a Royal Mounted Policeman?" Toad turned to look at me with those pleading, dark eyes and asked the question without saying a word. I stepped up to him placing my hand on his shoulder, thinking to myself, (You have grown up so fast. My God, you are taller than I am.) I said, "There is no more I can say to you or teach you my Son. You have chosen the path you want to follow and I will not stop you nor ask you not to go. You have to do what your heart tells you to do. I am so proud of you and I know your mother has always been proud of you. No matter where you go your mother's spirit will be with you to protect you and I will always have you in my heart."

Grizzly then stepped to Toad also and said, "You have become like a son to me as well." He took off the belt that held his cherished Bowie Knife and handed it to him saying, "Just so you won't forget me." Grizzly grabbed Toad in those big arms of his, giving him a big Bear hug. Toad stepped back when Grizzly finally let go of him and said, "I have been so fortunate to have had 2 great fathers. Not too many can say that," and then he turned and stepped into the stirrup of his faithful "Muley." He looked at the constable smiling and said, "I'm ready. Where do I sign up?"

My feelings were all mixed up when he stepped out onto the porch, the next day, looking so tall and handsome in the new Red Jacket and blue pants uniform that he was given. He still wore the beaded neckband his mother had given him, refusing to take it off. Then using two hands he secured his hat on his head, stepped forward and took the oath of the Royal

Canadian Mounted Police; "To uphold the law of the land with honor in the name of the Canadian Royal Mounted Police." The Constable then handed him a badge and shook his hand. Toad smiled turning to look at his "Two Father's" and winked. I glanced at Grizzly and saw the tears in his eyes.

As he placed his foot in the stirrup of his Mule and swung up on his back, I heard one of the other Policemen laugh and say something about his horse having such long ears. Then Toad yelled back saying, "This long eared "horse" will still be going when those scrawny ponies of yours will have fallen behind." They all laughed.

Word got back to us that Toad had found the body of Cannibal in the spring, where he had been buried under tons of snow from an avalanche. I thought to myself, "That must have been a real disappointment for him because he had wanted to have the privilege of killing him face-to-face himself.

Over the years, word would get back to us about the young half-breed Blackfoot Indian Mounty known as "Captain Toad Lawson" who showed so much bravery in battle and his quest to bring justice for crimes on the innocent. He always brought back the criminal. One way or the other there would be no escaping.

Grizzly and I stayed at the trading post for many weeks helping to rebuild the buildings. I couldn't let go of all my memories of Running Water and developed the need for the Home Brew Whiskey from the still out in the back of the saloon. It helped me to ease the pain of her loss and to forget for just a few hours. Many nights Grizzly would have to come and carry me back to our camp putting me to bed. I never remembered any of that, as I had made it a practice of starting my day with whiskey and by night, I would pass out with an empty bottle by my bed.

On many nights, I would start a fight with one or more of the trappers or miners who would wander in. Grizzly was not much of a drinking man, but he would tag along with me. I think to try to keep me out of trouble. He understood my pain. One night, He finally, just got fed up with me and went back to our camp alone, leaving me to deal with my drunken rage alone. I had started a fight with a couple of miners and as they started taking turns, beating my ass. I was too drunk to stand to defend myself.

They were laughing and calling me all kinds of names as they dragged me outside and proceeded to beat and kick me after I was down, busting my ribs. Someone had ran to get Grizzly and when he saw those men kicking me, shoving my face in the mud, laughing and calling me names, he went crazy. He grabbed one of them, lifted him over his head, and threw him at the other one, toppling them both into the mud. He then drew out his knife and grabbed the one by his hair bending his head back and was about to cut his throat. He said in a loud voice, "You do not laugh at this man. You do not know him." Only the sound of a rifle stopped him.

The Post agent had a rifle in his hand yelling in a loud voice, "That's enough Grizzly. They have had enough fun for one night. Drop the knife. I do not want to have to shoot you my friend, but I will if I have to. Pick Aully up and get him out of here." Then he pointed the rifle at the two miners and told them, "I think it would be best for you to get on your horses and skedaddle out of here." Then in a loud voice he said, "Now git!" I will not be responsible for what Grizzly will do. I can only hold him for just so long." It did not take them long to get to their horses and galloped out of range of that rifle.

A couple of other miners walked over to Grizzly and as they gazed down at my wretched muddy body lying in the mud, one of them said, "we understand all of this, but we think it would be best for you to get Aully out of here. The memory of Running Water and that scaffold up there on that hill has sent him into a bottomless pit. He has a death wish he will never come back from as long as he stays here."

Grizzly could only nod his head as if to say he understood. They helped Grizzly carry me to our camp and put me to bed. By midmorning, I awoke and as I tried to get out of my bed-roll, the pain hit me like a rock. My head was throbbing and my ribs were more painful than anything I had ever had to endure. I tried to get to my knees and raise my body to my feet, but I was unable to move. As I fell to the floor yelling as the pain racked my body, I was helpless. Grizzly came into my tent and found me like that. He just sat down on the floor and watched me struggle. I yelled at him, "Hey, you Son of a Bitch help me get up," but he just continued to look at me.

I turned to look at his face, he was just staring back at me, and when he spoke again, He said something I will never forget as long as I live. "I have picked you up for the last time, my friend. I have my horse waiting outside, saddled and a packhorse loaded with what is my share of our gold, furs and supplies. I am headed for Fairbanks. Your share is packed in a bundle outside. I have purchased a pack animal from Charlie and Buddy is hobbled outside. You can saddle him and ride with me, but you will have to do it yourself.

If you can get yourself ready and in the saddle, you are

more than welcome to ride with me, but I am finished with this business of you drinking yourself into a black hole every night. I am no longer going to pick you up out of the mud. You will have to fight your own battles. I almost killed a man for no reason last night because of you and it will not happen again. You will need your tent and bedroll, but you will have to deal with that on your own."

"I have paid Charlie for the damage from last night but you owe him a liquor bill. I will not pay for that." Then he turned and as he bent to walk out the tent door, he looked back at me and said, "I loved her too, but I will not dishonor her memory like this," and then he was gone.

As I heard him ride away, the realization of what he said sank in. I could only bend my head down on the edge of my bedroll and the tears from the pain of these last weeks over-whelmed me. I was filled with shame and the grief of all I had lost flooded my memories.

First the loss of Tapping Bird. I had not given myself time to grieve for her. I had tried to be strong for everyone else. Then the unbearable loss of my beautiful Running Water. I did not know I could love anyone as much as I had loved her. I do not know how to live without her. Seeing Toad ride away, leaving an empty hole in my heart and feeling the weight of my loneliness, I wept uncontrollable. My body weak from my pain, I slipped into unconsciousness across my bed.

I could not know how long I lay there, only to be awakened by the sound of her voice, "Aully." Again she called my name, "Aully, wake up my love." I opened my eyes and turned my face to see who was calling my name.

I rose and turned to look in the direction of the voice. The room was dark, but from the open doorway, there was a dim light. I strained to see who it was and then the voice came again in a whisper, "Aully, you must go, it is time." By now, I was sitting up. I reached out, but not able to touch her I cried, "Running Water you have come for me." The voice said again, "You will have to go on alone; there is much for you to do yet. My spirit will be with you always," and then she was gone. "No, no, don't leave me," I cried. I sat there for a long time deep in my thoughts. We had so little time.

Tapping Bird, Toad, and Running Water came into my life when I needed them and I loved every minute I had with them. It was priceless and no amount of gold could have given me the happiness they did. I would give all the gold I had just to have one minute more with them, to tell them how precious they were to me.

My thoughts were interrupted by the sound of Buddy as he pawed the ground outside my tent. Then I remembered what Grizzly said about him being hobbled outside. I painfully got to my feet and stumbled outside. The night was still as the first sign of light was beginning to rise over the trees. I could feel the crust of the blood on my face as I gazed at my blood covered hands. For the first time I really felt dirty and needed to wash all the filth from weeks of not caring about how I looked. My very soul reeked of the stench.

Turning towards the river I slowly walked to the river edge, shedding each piece of clothing as I walked. Naked, I walked into the cold black water letting myself sink into its black obis, waking up every pore of my aching body. I stayed there for a long time until I could not feel anything. Half wanting not to surrender to the reality of living as my lungs were bursting for air I raised to the surface. I gasped for the fresh air that filled my lungs with life. Reaching the edge of the river, I dragged myself onto the grassy bank. I lay there briefly begging the cold night air to clear my head.

As I struggled to stand, I noticed Buddy hobbled, watching me as the packhorse tied to the tree also waited. On the ground next to the tent was all my gear. Then his words came back to me. "I loved her too," he had said, "but I will not dishonor her memory this way." It never occurred to me that he had loved her too, never letting it show. It must have been hard for him all those years to keep his feelings hidden. He was so wise and I respected everything he said to me as I gazed into the water at my reflexion. He was right. How could I disrespect her like this? She deserved much more.

I turned and walked to the horses, hugged and pet them, letting them know that I had not forgotten them. "Just give me a little more time." I said, "Tomorrow we will start a new life, but tonight I must sleep. I am so tired." I untied the packhorse I now called "Sugar Cane" She looked like a piece of candy with her red and white smeared stripes. She didn't look like any paint horse I had ever seen before, but she had a gentle face and intelligent eyes. "I think I will like her a lot," I thought to myself as I hobbled her and turned her lose with Buddy. Then I dragged all my gear into the tent collapsing my naked body onto my bedroll and was immediately asleep.

I must have slept all the next day and night because I awoke just as the sun was coming over the horizon and shining through the trees. I carefully got to my feet and walked naked out to the river's edge, looking at my reflexion in the water. Only this time I really took a good look at myself. I saw someone

I did not recognize. A dirty bearded man looked back at me with blood shot eyes and a bruised swollen face. "What had I let myself become?" I thought of Mamma and wondered what she would have thought of me if she could see me now. I bet she would have given me quite a tongue-lashing. That's funny, I have not thought about Mamma and Daddy or the ranch for a long time. I promised myself I would write them a letter and tell them about my adventures.

I dug my knife and straight razor from my gear and returned to the river where I began the grueling job of cutting my long dirty hair and shaving off all my whiskers, letting them drop in a pile at my feet. Then I looked at my naked body touching all the cuts and bruises, again asking myself, "What have I done to myself?"

I walked down the street after I dressed in the same dirty clothes I had on the night before, leading Buddy and Sugar Cane behind me. I had to smile as I watched everyone who knew me look at me questioning, wondering who I was. They didn't recognize me. When I stepped through the door of the Trading Post the agent just glanced up at me, greeting me with, "Hello." Then he started to say, "What can I do . . .," and then he stopped and stared.

"Well I'll be damned, Aully is that you?" I had to laugh. "Yes, it's me and if you can pick your jaw off the floor I would like to do some business with you this morning. I need to buy some new duds, and I would like to apologize for all the times I came in here and made a fool of myself. I am ashamed of that." He shook his head and said, "Aully we all understood and there is no need for you to say anything."

I changed there in the store, throwing all my old clothes in the trash barrel as I walked out the door. Then I walked down to the saloon and as I walked up to the bar, Charlie greeted me and asked, "What'll yah have?" I looked at him and said, "Charlie, I don't want a drink. I had my last one the other night. I came here to pay the tab that I owe you. I also want to say I am sorry for the mess I made in here when I started that fight with those miners."

He looked at me for a minute and said, "Aully?" I nodded, and he continued, "I don't know if you owe me anything, but just seeing you the way you look now is worth everything you owe me. It's paid in full." I put out my hand and shook his. "I probably won't be coming this way again, but you have been a good friend and I will not forget you." I then turned and walked out the door.

Slowly I walked up to the scaffold where she was resting and looked up. "You probably don't recognize me in all these new duds, but I think you would like the new look, all clean shaven and smart looking. I want you to know I have no regrets about you and me. You are and always will be the love of my life and I will cherish every minute for the rest of my life. It just ended too soon. I wasn't ready."

"Thank you for showing what a real love could be. I am releasing you to go to your people now. You do not need to worry about me. I am going to be okay. I am going to find my friend Grizzly, and beg him to give me another chance. I won't be back this way again, but I know you will also be on your own journey with your people." Pausing for a second to let it all sink in, I continued, "Goodbye, my love. I love you." I turned and not looking back mounted Buddy and rode in the direction I was sure Grizzly had gone.

Jason Aaron Bradford the 3rd

I traveled fast for the next 2 days looking for signs along the river. I saw where he had camped and about 30 miles from Fairbanks I could smell the smoke of his campfire. Tying the horses, I crept slowly closer to make sure it was him. He was squatting by his fire stirring a pot of beans, deep in his own thoughts. When he saw the figure walking out of the trees, startled, he grabbed his rifle aiming it at me. I yelled at him, "Hey, Grizzly don't shoot. It's me Aully." He did not recognize me at first without my beard and all cleaned up. I wasn't wearing the Coon Skin cap or the Bear Skin coat. He continued to point the rifle at me and then I yelled again, "It's me, Aully."

He stared in wonder as I stepped into the light of the fire. Then he broke into a huge smile. "What have you done to yourself? You're all cleaned up." I laughed and said, "I couldn't stand the smell any longer so I took a bath. Maybe you have become accustomed to being stinky for too long because you could use a bath with some strong lye soap yourself." "Hey Mr. Uppity, be careful. What the hell took you so long?" Then he grabbed me, giving me a big bear hug, crushing my ribs in the process. As I grimaced and moaned, he remembered my broken ribs. He let go spreading his hands apart saying, "I'm sorry. I forgot about that.

"I will go get my animals, and then we will eat some of that stew you got there. I have something to talk to you about.

I might be looking for a good business partner." Later as we sat by the fire drinking his strong, coffee I began to tell him of my plan. "You once told me you had been a captain on a ship spending most of your young life as a sailor. Why did you leave it?"

His story was much like my own. He had a wandering heart and just wanted to see what else there was out there, indicating with a wave of his arm. "I was bored and I had seen everything there was to see, been to every port that could be visited from a ship. I wanted to see what was on the other side of the ocean." I asked him, "Do you ever miss it?" "Yah, sometimes. Then he paused for a moment, then looking at me he asked. "Where are you going with this, Aully?"

"Well, I came from a beautiful ranch in the Rocky Mountains of Colorado and it would have been the perfect place to spend the rest of my life herding cattle, raising a family, and just living out a dream life. Like you, I was restless to see more and I wanted to be a mountain man, so I left."

"We have trapped, we have panned for gold, and we are richer then I could have ever dreamed of." Do I miss the ranch? Yes very much at times. I would love to see my Mamma and Daddy and my little sister, Maude. Do I regret my decision to come to the Canadian territory? Not for one minute." I paused, and then I continued, "There is one thing I do know about, and that is cattle, and cattle means food. There is a big demand for beef in Alaska with all the miners and now settlers moving in with their families. Someone has to ship those cattle north on a ship. That is where you come in, my friend."

Grizzly looked at me as if I had lost my mind and then he started that slow smile as the thought began to make sense to him, and realizing where I was going with this. He leaned back with his hands on one of his knees, teetering back and forth, gazing into the empty space around him. "Well, we do have a lot of money we don't know what to do with, and my friend won't be spending it at the saloon anymore. I also know all there is to know about cargo ships. Actually, I was a ship captain and I have hauled just about everything there is to haul, including cattle all over the world. I think we should check this out a lot more, as soon as we reach Fairbanks. We might need a friend in the bank."

"Well, it just so happens I stopped in and talked to Jack Cord before I left Fort Selkin. We had a very interesting conversation about money. Just so happens, he has another bank in Fairbanks. He said he would be heading there in a couple of days and for us to stop in when we get there and see him." "Does that mean I will have to take a bath like you?" I just laughed and nodded, with my head lowered, looking at him without raising my head.

Next morning, Grizzly was up early. He had stripped to his skin, scrubbed his body, shaved his beard and cut his hair. I could not help but think to myself, "I had better keep an eye on the big guy; there will be many women taking a second look at this handsome fellow." He had left just enough of his mustache to give him that distinguished look. Almost as if he could read my mind, he smiled and said, "For your information, I was quite a ladies man once." "Well," I replied, "Now you are a very rich ladies' man and there will be a lot of women out there just waiting for the chance to snag a man like you." "Don't worry about me, my friend, I know all about those women, I have already been down that road."

"There is a lot I do not know about you. By the way, what is your name?" "Jason Aaron Bradford the 3rd. I was educated at Bradford College in England. Named after my very wealthy Grandfather the first. He also owned the shipping company I sailed for. I didn't really need to search for gold to strike it rich. I already was rich." I couldn't speak at first. "I wouldn't have guessed that about you," I said, when I was finally able to speak. He continued to say, "I want you to know we will not be using my families' wealth. We will be on our own." Will that make a difference?" I reached out my hand saying, "Agreed, partner." He took my hand and smiled saying, "Partner." That was the only agreement we ever had to make. A handshake sealed the deal.

Our first stop when we got to Fairbanks was to the Jack Cord Bank of Fairbanks. We had a long talk with him. At which time he said he would like to buy into our business, but he would want to be a silent partner if that would be all right with us. His main interest would be to arrange the market for the cattle and supplies we could get from Anchorage. There was a new road being built along the east wall of the 20,000-foot Mount McKinley to Fairbanks. He said he was planning to open another bank in Anchorage, which would make a good headquarters for the newly established shipping and cattle ranch of our new business. He also said it would be a good idea to name it. At the same time we said, "We kind of like the name, "The Shipping Company."

By the end of the first year, we had a 3,000-acre cattle ranch on the peninsula at Douglas Mountain and Jason had arranged with his family in England to purchase three barges for shipping supplies and cattle. We were on our way to becoming the wealthiest shipping tycoons in Alaska. In the next three years, Jack had located a firm that was based out of Skagway who were already making shipments of supplies to Dawson up the railroad trail. We supplied the cattle and they supplied the canned goods that came from Seattle. It was a good arrangement all the way around. Jason met and married a nice woman and was settling down into a comfortable family life, for which he was well suited.

He knew all there was to know about the shipping business and with Jacks help; we had invested into much of the progress of the Alaska territory. For the next 6 years, we were very sure that nothing could hurt us or interfere with our progress. We became very comfortable with our wealth.

That spring the weather had been very dry and the drought was wide spread all over the country. There had not been as much snowfall as in the previous years. The end of May a fire broke out in a dentist office in Fairbanks and before it could be contained, it had destroyed all of the three banks in town and every business was wiped out. Fortunately the sawmill cut the lumber, that was available in that area, most of the businesses had rebuilt if only as a temporary structure. The Banks however, would not be able to be back in business for quite some time. It took a couple of days before word got back to Jason and myself, that Jack's bank was one of the ones destroyed in the fire.

Jacks attempts to get all the contracts and legal documents, which were in his safe, were futile. He died as a result. He had tried to run through the middle of the flames but was so badly burned that he never recovered. His death was a devastating blow to our shipping business, as all our contracts were stored in his safe along with the records of our investments.

We had deposited a large amount of our money in the bank in Anchorage and we knew we would just have to go to our investors, as they would have duplicates of our contracts. We were able to recoup most of them.

After a conversation, Jason and I agreed that without Jack's genius financial advice we would not have been where we were today. After his death, things just were not the same. We just could not get up the enthusiasm we had before. We had no interest in continuing.

We tried to make sense of this news and one day as we sat in our office, I began to talk. "I don't know how you feel about it, Jason, but so much has happened to me in the last 10 years. We both have fulfilled our dreams. I wanted to be a mountain man and I did that. Then we struck it rich in the gold fields and now we have become rich shipping tycoons, but we have had to pay a high price for all this."

"You told me once that you wanted to see what was on the other side of that mountain. I paused then continued. "Well what do you think of it now?" Again, I paused for a second, and not needing an answer, I continued. My heart was heavy and I had to say all that I was feeling. Lowering my head, I continued, "Oh, Jason, there was so much loss for me to bear. I wonder if it was all worth it. Our dear friend Jack is gone and I feel such a heavy loss, He played a large part of my family's beginnings and probably is why I am here. I have never been able to get over my loss of Running Water and I have never felt as lonely as I do now. I feel I need to return to the wilderness and find the peace I felt there. Maybe I will find some semblance of happiness again. I would like to find Toad, talk to him, and see how he is doing. I guess what I am so clumsily saying is that I want out of this way of life. I want to go back to my "Roots" and start over. Maybe then, I can find a purpose to living. I don't need to be rich. I don't really want the money. I don't need it and it hasn't made me any happier." Jason sat there and listened intently to every word his friend was saying and when Aully stopped, he began to speak,

"My brother, I have watched you all these years and I was hoping you would find another woman to replace Running Water, to help you ease the pain and grief you carried in your heart. You had a rare love that bonded the two of you together for life, that could never be broken, and I should have known that no one could have eased that pain. I have envied you that. I also felt the grief of her death. I also loved her, but I had no way to let you know how I felt. I was alone in it, but I was sure she knew how I felt, although, she never let on or encouraged it. She only had her love for you. You are my brother and my dearest friend. You always will be. I just wanted you to be happy. I love my wife, but not in the way, I loved Running Water and I probably never will be able to. I also have been thinking about all of this. I did not know how you felt, but I would like to take my family back to England to live. It would be a good life for them with the best schools.

I have had my adventure and I am not getting any younger. I feel age creeping up on me these days. I do not want to wander in the wilderness again and I don't want to have to worry about making money. We have enough to live very well in England. I want my children to be educated in the best schools, and they need to learn about their ancestors and know who they are and where they came from. My parents are very old now and still alive. I want them to see their only grandchildren."

Arrangements were made to sell all the cattle and the Shipping Company. The 3000-acre ranch was donated to the Territory of Alaska with the stipulation that it would be established as a nature reserve. I could not visualize it being anything else.

As I stood on the pier and watched as the ship pull out of the port, the loneliness was unbearable. I knew I would never see my friend again. It was more than I could bear as I tried to choke back the tears that came, without shame. "Well, Hotshot," I said out loud to myself. "Now what are you going to do?" As I turned and walked away, a thought came to me. "I wonder if old Buddy is still alive." I had to laugh at that and then aloud I said to myself, "I think I will look for another big Bay like Jake."

I found another bay Stallion that I named Mac. He wasn't Jake, but he was a good strong horse and very intelligent. I was also able to purchase a good pack mule I named Casey, she was pretty as any I had ever seen; steady, gentle, and a willingness to do whatever was asked of her. Riding away from all the business of the coast, I looked back for the last time at all I was leaving behind.

All the old chapters of my life were ending there and a new one was to begin. I had many different emotions about it, but I was also excited about the new adventure I was embarking on. There was that same feeling of excitement I had when I left the ranch so many years ago. I almost felt like the youth I had been then. I did not have any idea where it would lead me, but I am a lot smarter now and could hardly wait to get back to the wilderness.

I traveled along the coast, crossing rivers and marshes, seeing hundreds of caribou grazing on the plush Tundra. I would only watch them not having any desire to shoot one of these gigantic animals. My heart raced, as I felt like the boy once again, when I would herd the cattle and touch the antlers of the huge elk that would be grazing along with the cattle. I camped along the river tributaries, catching the huge Salmon as they made their way upstream to spawn. Many times, I had to hide from the bear, who were also fishing in the same rapids where I was camped.

I was anxious to get to Skagway, Canada where the headquarters for The Royal Canadian Mounted Police were located. I wanted to find Toad and was told, they would be able to tell me where He might be. When I walked into their headquarters and stepped up to a desk where the Constable was sitting, I asked if they knew how I could get hold of Toad. They asked if I meant Captain Toad Lawson. I did not have to say more, as everyone knew him and it was obvious he was held in high esteem. I felt my heart race when they said his name. It made me feel very proud. "Captain Toad Lawson. It sounded good," I thought to myself.

When I asked again, where I might find him, they said, He had taken a small troop and was heading for the high Stewart River District east of Dawson. They continued to tell me of a band of renegade Cree Indians and a group of outlaw French trappers that had raided a peaceful Blackfoot village in the Northwest Territory. They had attacked while the braves were out hunting. These renegades were raiding the small encampments of the Indians, butchering, raping, and killing all the women and children. This is a real bad bunch of killers, especially when they are mixed bloods like that.

The Cree Indians are the hated enemy of the Blackfeet and I am afraid there will be a war once the Blackfoot Confederacy recovers from these raids. These Renegades came from the plains area and have left behind a blood trail wherever they go.

Captain Lawson said it reminded him of another bunch from a few years back that called themselves "The Cannibal Gang." The difference is that Cannibal ate their victims, they didn't just kill them. This gang rides with a "Breed" who paints his face red, with black circles around his eyes and is as bad as any man can be.

A feeling of nausea overwhelmed me as I asked, "How long ago did the troop leave and which direction were they going?" He told me, "A week ago. They were going to stop in Dawson first to get more ammo and supplies. You could stop there, the Constable would be able to tell you more." "I think I will just mosey in that direction and see if they could use some help," I told him as I left.

I headed for Mac and Casey who were grazing in the yard near the headquarters. After checking their pack, I remembered seeing a Henry rifle in the Post store, so I decided to buy it and get more ammunition for my Winchester. It wouldn't hurt to be armed with more then I need, just in case. The Henry Rifle; I heard was the most accurate long distance rifle there was and it had a one shot kill. That was good because I would only need one shot.

I did not waste any time getting back on the trail and by mid-afternoon I had traveled a long distance from Skagway. I talked to a couple of miners on my way and they said they had seen the Mounties; and they seemed to be in a hurry. They stopped just long enough to warn us to be on the lookout for a band of renegade Cree Indians and French outlaws riding together and to be sure to post sentries at our camp. Every fiber of my being told me to hurry, so I did not waste time getting to Dawson and the headquarters.

The officer in charge did not know for sure where the troop was, but he said, "If they were heading along the Stewart River it is rough terrain and the closer they get to the mountains the rougher it gets.

"Yes," I remembered those mountains." It sent a remembered feeling of foreboding through me. He continued, "We still have some snow on the tops that does not always melt right away." I decided to go to the post and get myself some good winter underwear and a heavy coat and cap before I started up. After checking the animals and making sure they were trail worthy, I was back on the trail heading for the high country along the Stewart River.

By nightfall, I had traveled about 22 miles and by now, the forest was becoming more dense. It was hard to stay on the river's edge, making me lead the horses along the narrow ledge, and as the trail led into a clearing I took out my binoculars scoping the area. About a mile out, I could see the red coats of the Mounties as they were crawling to the edge of the ledge. One Mountie was holding the horses and trying to keep them quiet and still. I scoped the ravine and saw the outlaws below. They did not seem to be doing much more than waiting for something.

I moved closer to get a better look and as I continued to scope the hillside above the Mounties, I saw a flash and then I saw them. The Cree renegades had sneaked along the ridge above the troops and were getting into position for an ambush. Those men in the valley below were set up as a decoy to throw the troops off.

I searched for Toad again. Finding Him, I noticed he had filled out more and gotten taller. He had a mustache that made him look older. He was no longer that skinny kid I had said goodbye to so long ago. Then the panic set in as I contemplated how I was going to let them know they were being set up. I could not tell how many renegades there were, but they were very well versed in the tactics of ambush.

The Cree were known for their knowledge of warfare tactics. They had a reputation as a vicious band of killers. They had been fighting the Blackfoot Indians forever, neither able to defeat the other. The Blackfoot Confederacy were also skilled horseman and would use those battle tactics to their advantage. They were also known as the greatest fighting force in battle and were never defeated. Many of their fighting tactics were later to be integrated by the army for hunting and fighting their enemies.

It made sense why the Cree attacked the Blackfoot village while most of the braves were out on a hunting expedition. The big question was why they teamed up with the French Trappers. A question that might never be answered.

Somehow, I had to warn the troops, but I was too far away to fire a shot without giving away my own position. I knew I had to fire a shot. I quickly ran to get into position and was able to get to within 100 yards of this ambush. I had no choice. I had to make my presence known even though it would direct the enemy's attention away from the troops for a while although, they might just come after me, which did not frighten me, I was ready for them.

With the Henry Rifle, I crept to the edge of the trees, aiming at the biggest warrior I could get in my sights, but before I could pull the trigger, a shot rang out and I saw Toad fall. He took a shot in the back, killing him instantly. I sighted in trying to find the killer, who had been hiding back from the rest, but I had not seen him before it was too late. He was dressed in buckskin and over top; He had on a bearskin vest, which had been inlaid with bear claws. His face was painted red covering his lips hiding his features with painted black circles surrounding his eyes. He was a frightening sight to behold.

I had heard about the Negro, Apache half breed. It was said he came from the Mexico high country. His hair was greased down and hung loose next to his face.

As I raised the Henry to my shoulder, I placed my scope on him and pulled the trigger. I missed, as my hands were shaking so bad I couldn't hold the rifle still. All I could see was Toad lying there in his own blood. All Hell broke loose after the first shot was fired. No one had spotted me yet. I was shooting wild, hitting only a couple of the renegades. As quick as the shooting started it stopped. There was silence all around. There were renegades lying dead on the ledge above and four of the mounted Police were dead. The wounded had crawled behind some boulders trying to get out of line of fire. The shooting was over and all of the Indians had vanished into the forest, escaping back into the hills. I looked for the Red Faced Man hoping I had hit him, but he was gone. I figured he had run as soon as the first shots were fired.

I got back on Mac riding like a Mad Man, with Casey following along behind, as best as she could. Jumping off Mac, I ran to Toad and rolled him over taking him in my arms holding him close to my chest.

One of the police stumbled over to me, holding the side where he had been shot. Touching my shoulder, he said, "I don't know who you are, but we have to get out of here and take our men, wounded or not with us. They will be back to collect all their bootie and if they find any of our men they will do terrible things to the bodies, and we cannot have that. For now they are confused about where that extra gun fire was coming from, but they will surely be back." He repeated. "We have to hurry and get out of these mountains."

We rode through the night hurrying back to Dawson with the dead and the wounded. By morning as we entered the Fort, word had already preceded us. Many of the Mounties had come to meet us making sure we had protection and they took over the rescue, taking the reins of the horses carrying the bodies. I saw Muley with Toads body wrapped in a blanket draped over his back. I followed them as the bodies were gently laid on the ground in a row in front of the Headquarters.

I couldn't leave him. I stood at his feet looking down at the mound not able to shed a tear. When the captain walked up beside me he said, "I feel this man was someone special to you." "Yes," I said. "He is my son. I am Aully Lawson." He smiled and said, "I have heard a lot about you and a man named Grizzly." I smiled, remembering, saying, "He was the only boy who could say he had two fathers. He was special and it took two of us to raise him, but he turned out good. We were very proud to be called his Father's."

Captain Toad Lawson was buried with honors in Dawson two days later. They handed me a small gold jewelry box and inside was a gold Medallion tied with a ribbon and a patch that read "Canadian Royal Mounted Police, with the inscription that read "Medal of Honor for Bravery. Captain Toad Lawson."

I looked at it and thought, "Not much for a life, but I guess a life remembered is better than not at all. I made a vow to myself and to Toad, "I will avenge you for this Life taken and there will be no honor in their death.

Final Revenge

I walked into the headquarters of the Royal Canadian Mounted Police without hesitation asked for the man in charge of recruiting. A tall mustached man dressed in a red uniform stepped to the counter and asked what he could do for me. I told him, "I want to sign up." After looking me over from top to bottom he said, "If you will wait for just a minute, I'll get you someone you can talk to." I told him, " to make it Snappy, as I didn't have time to mess around. I am in a hurry.

He left and in just a few minutes, a man I recognized from a long time ago came to the counter and said, "I believe I know you. You are Aully Lawson aren't you?" "Yes, that is my name." I answered. "Toad was the man I recruited after the death of your wife. You are his father." The Captain continued. I am sorry about the death of your son. He paused, receiving no acknowledgment from me, He continued, "Well, Aully, what is this about? I understand you want to sign up and become a Mounted Policeman?" "What is so hard to understand about me wanting to sign up?" I replied. "Well you don't just come in and sign up. You have to go to training and sign a pledge first." I interrupted him and said. "You didn't ask my son to go to training when you came to him to join up, and to go after The Cannibal Gang. Why should this be any different?" "Let me explain something to you."

"First let's get this straight; I have no intention of training for anything. I am going to go kill a cold-blooded murderer. You should have done it a long time ago before he ambushed and murdered my son and half his company in cold blood. Now, I will get your blessing to do it legally, or I will do what you should have done a long time ago, illegally I might add. I don't much care which way I do it, but I am going to do it with or without your blessings."

The captain looked at me for just a minute then he reached into a drawer and pulled out a gold and silver badge that read "Royal Canadian Mounted Police, with the word Captain written in it. He ran his thumb over the lettering on the face and said. "This is the badge worn proudly by your son. This also makes you Captain Aully Lawson "I guess I don't need to waste your time or mine to ask you to raise your right hand, do I?" "I will say this though; I wish I were going with you." I looked at him and said. "No you don't." He had a slight smile on his lips when he said. "This is as bad a gang of killers as you will ever encounter. You have my blessing to kill each and every one of them in any means you see fit, and "off the record" Dead or alive, means don't bother to bring any of them back alive." He paused then he said, "This conversation never happened, you understand?" With that, he handed me the Badge, offering me his hand. I took it and then turned and walked out the door. I stuck the badge on my shirt, again I saying to myself. "Ok, Hotshot, now what?" "You are a Royal Canadian Mounted Policeman, what were you thinking?" "Toad, that's what. So go kill yourself a half breed killer!"

I walked to my horses and began to sort through all my gear. There were many things I wouldn't need and I wanted to eliminate the unnecessary gear. I was planning to ride fast and my animals would not need to carry more then was necessary. I made sure I had plenty of warm clothes and enough ammunition to kill an army. I did not know how far into the interior I would have to go, but I was going to avenge Toad's death if it took forever or I died trying.

Then I sat down and decided to write a will. I wrote a letter to Maude and one to Mamma and Daddy. That was the hardest thing I had to do. I tried to tell them about the past few years, but I did not say what I was about to do. I put an entry into my journal about it. Mamma would never forgive me if I did not keep it up to date and as honest as I could be about it. I had to laugh about that, and then I put my letters in a sealed envelope giving all this paperwork to the Captain to mail, putting my journal in my saddlebag. As I rode out of the courtyard, I noticed the Mounties had stood in a line for me to pass through. Some just reached out to touch my horses and me. Some said, as I passed by them, "Go get 'em for Captain Lawson and God speed."

I headed up the winding treacherous Stewart River, veering off to climb high above the roaring water below. Many times, I would have to lead the horses, the ledge being so narrow that one slip and we would all tumble 1000 feet below to sure death. Mac and Casey were seasoned mountain horses, instinctively knowing the Mountains; I had no reason to worry.

One night, I had camped just at the mouth of the narrow gorge and as I was preparing to bed down for the night, I could hear the cry of a mountain lion in the distance. Each time the cry would get closer as the night progressed. I kept my pistol by my side. Just as I was kneeling to put another log on the fire she lunged and caught my jacket sleeve as I side stepped just in time, swinging the log in my hand, hitting her in the head as she passed by me. She fell in the dirt dazed, at the feet of my trusty Casey, startling her. She jumped and turned at the same time, eyes blazing, as if to say, "You Son of a Bitch, how dare you disturb me while I am eating.

What happened next was beyond anything I could have imagined. That cat did not have a chance against the wild beast that was ready for her. Casey lunged at her and with her lip curled back; she took a chunk out of that cats head, lopping off her ear. The cat lay in the dirt for just a minute stunned, then, struggling to get back on her feet, she still had some fight left in her, but by then I had recovered my pistol and fired a shot. She fell face first to the ground, dead. All this happening in less than a minute.

I walked over to the lion and kicked it once to make sure she was dead. I turned to look at Casey. She looked at the cat and snorted then lowered her head and was back to munching on the sweet grass at her feet, totally unaffected by all of this. While I had been sweating bullets, from the excitement of everything, I thought to myself, I really could have used some moral support and concern from my fighting mate. However, Casey was as unconcerned as she could be. She raised her head just long enough and looked at me as if to say, "What's the problem?" It was all in a day's work for her and I had to laugh at myself.

Next morning when I slipped her a bit more oats for her breakfast, she didn't balk at all. I skinned and cleaned the hide. Rolling it up, tucking it in with my bedroll for the time being, thinking I might have to use it later to barter with. I had fixed me a cup of coffee and was eating a hardtack as we rode out of the gorge. We dropped in altitude, leaving the high country behind. I was anxiously looking for signs of riders.

After 4 days of steady riding, that familiar feeling of uneasiness started to creep in. I had learned years ago to listen to my instincts. Even Mac had begun to show signs that something was amiss. He normally walked relaxed with his head lowered looking where his feet were going, but he had raised his head, with his ears twitching listening for that silent sound. Then a low rumble would come from deep in his throat telling me to stay alert. I had found that if you watch your animals they would tell you things you might not notice, like a hidden danger.

I slowly pulled my Winchester out of its scabbard and lay it across my saddle in front of me, cocking it as I did. For the next 100 yards I walked slowly watching and listening for the sound of a twig or crunch of horse's hooves as they walked on the dry grass. Just as we rounded a bend in the path, Mac raised his head, a rumble coming from his throat. We heard the faint answer just as "He" stepped out of the trees.

The familiar figure I had dreamed of from so many years ago, sitting tall on his Black Stallion, was the dark skinned Indian of my youth. The one they called "Chief Black Raven."

Mac raised his head arching his neck as if to challenge this Stallion, but he never accepted the challenge. Not a muscle moved and for a short time, neither of us spoke. As I looked at him, I remembered the familiar beaded leggings and the large knife still in his sheaf, the hand woven blanket draped over the back of this gigantic beauty of a horse. The man had aged some, but I thought to myself, so have you. His long black hair had a few streaks of gray, but that fierceness was still there. He was no less magnificent as when I was a young boy.

I spoke first. "Do you remember "Boy Who Touches Elk?" For a moment, I thought I might have been wrong and then a smile began to form on his face. "Yes, I remember. You are older." Then he added, "You have come a long way from your homeland. Why are you in these mountains?" "I have a long story to tell, but for now I will say I have come to kill a half breed Indian." I replied. Silence and then he continued, "This half breed you speak of does he wear a Bear Skin robe with bear claws on its neck, the one with the painted, "Red Face?" "Yes he is the one." "I too am searching for this Man; He will be my victory to kill."

I immediately was angered by his statement and thinking to myself, "Who was he, that he should take my revenge from me? Challenging him, I said. "I have lost my son to the hands of this killer. I have no intention of letting anyone else take this honor from me."" We sat in silence looking at each other both thinking about our own reasons for wanting the honor of killing this monster.

Then he spoke. "I am Chief Black Raven. Chief of the Blackfoot Confederacy. I have traveled a long way to avenge the massacre of my village by this man and his renegade band of Cree and French trappers. I will show no mercy to anyone who will stand in my way as well." I knew he meant every word he spoke. I responded, "I to, am on a journey to avenge the killing of my son and the four Mounties this gang of killers ambushed. The Red Faced Breed and the rest of his renegades shot them like the cowards they are, in an ambush, shooting them all in the back. He is the one who shot my son and I mean to cut his heart out. My name is Aully Lawson and my son was a Captain in the Royal Canadian Mounted Police." His name was Captain Toad Lawson."

When I said his name, Chief Black Raven looked at me and said, "I have heard of this man, he was a brave and honorable man. Perhaps we should travel together and the one who kills Red Face will kill with no mercy for both of us." "You are a wise man," I thought to myself. I was happy to have him as my ally rather than my enemy. I was sure he would be a formidable enemy.

For days we traveled far into the high Rocky Mountains of the Northern Canadian Territory, following a trail that seemed to have no end. We would have to stop because of the altitude and thin air. The horses were having a hard time as well, with the packs they were carrying. Just as we reached the summit of 16,000 feet, we could smell the smoke from a campfire and then the sound of gunfire; then there was silence. We were too far away to be of any help to whoever was there. The sound of the rifles would carry for miles as it echoed through the canyons. We would have to go over some very dangerous terrain to get there in time to be of any help.

Black Raven motioned for me to be very cautious from now on. If it were the Red Face Gang, they more than likely would have scouts out. He felt we were close to the end of our journey; we could not make any mistakes. My heart was pounding so loud with anticipation; I was afraid they could hear it and give away our position. I wanted to see the Red Faced Monster and I wanted to make him suffer.

That night we did not have a fire, eating jerky and hard tack. As we sat in darkness, Black Raven began to speak, "Our camp was running low on food, so my braves and I decided to go hunt for the Moose that would sustain our people for the winter months. We were gone for two moons, killing many moose. As we came into our village, no one came to greet us. We saw the burned teepees and hides that had been dragged all over the ground and trampled. We saw the children who had been mutilated, with their heads, arms, and legs cut off. I ran to my teepee where my wife and two daughters were, but as I entered I saw them lying in their own blood. Their naked bodies had been ravaged and they had been raped. My wife's belly had been cut open and her intestines were lying in the ground next to her."

He continued to talk, telling of the other horrible things that had been done to his people. I stopped listening. it was more than I could stand to hear. He told of the next days when the people who escaped performed the burial rites for the dead. Many of the peoples from other camps came to help and the wailing of grief was unbearable.

"The Red Coat Policeman came, saying his name was Captain Toad Lawson; saying they were on the trail of a gang of renegade Cree Indians and French Trappers who rode with a red faced half breed. He said he was sure these horrible killings were the work of the same gang as the ones he was trailing. They had been raiding and killing all along; the Saskatchewan Territory and they were being chased and hunted by every division of the Mounted Police."

"If they are brought into the jails in Dawson they will be hanged." He looked at me and continued to say, "I promise you if I catch them first there will be no trial and I will deal with them fast and final in my own way."

I understood why Black Raven wanted this murderer

himself to deal with in the manner of the Blackfoot way. All of this gang would suffer unimaginable torture for many hours before they would mercifully die. I knew there would be no one to stand in his way, but as for me, I vowed to him that I would hold this "Bastard" as he cut his heart out while he was still alive.

Now we had an agreement. Whichever one of us caught this renegade, the other one would hold him while the other cuts his heart out. Neither one of us gave any thought to the rest of the gang we would have to kill to get to Red Face. We were not able to focus on anything but our hatred for this monster, and that was to become a problem. We did not think about the 15 plus more men in this gang we would have to go through to get to our objective.

Next morning we were back on the trail. We followed the river for about 2 miles when we spotted the first body. It was half in and half out of the water. It appeared as though he had tried to run and was shot in the back falling into the current and floating down river, only to get tangled in the fallen trees along the shoreline. We did not stay to bury the body, only looking but kept on riding. We did not want to slow our progress, we were sure the gang was not too far ahead of us.

That feeling crept into my body as I noticed Mac raise his head and his ears were twitching straining to hear the sound of the horses ahead of us on the trail. Black Raven slowed his horse, motioning for me to go into the trees and stay still. He continued ahead for a short distance and then he was lost in the forest as well. I held my horses, holding my hands over their nostrils, sensing there was danger close, neither horse made a sound, nor did they move. Heads high, they were watching for the riders as well.

Off to the right of me, on the other side of the river, we heard voices; a mixture of The Cree and French language. Five Cree and two trappers rode into the clearing. They were looking into the river as if they were looking for something along the riverbank. Red Face was not with them. Just as they reached the body of the man, a chill ran through me remembering our tracks in the mud. In the distance, a rifle shot was heard, distracting them. They stopped looking for whatever it was they were looking for, and spun their horses around, galloping back the way they had come. I let my breathe out slowly and waited a few minutes, then walked out of the trees and into the clearing.

Black Raven was already standing there watching in their direction. I asked, "What do you suppose they were looking for?" "Us, I think," was his reply. "The Cree are very good at knowing their surrounding and by now they must know they are being dogged. I know I would, if I were them. From now on we must make a plan." I had been thinking about that myself and I suspected there are more men in their gang then we had thought. "What do you think we should do?" I asked, "We can't just go charging into their camp with guns blazing." "Maybe we will have to start to make their band smaller; enough for us to handle." He said. I understood what he was getting at and nodded my agreement.

As the days wore on we continued to follow them and when one was alone we would pick him off silently, Black Raven with his knife hitting him in the throat so he could not be able to make a sound, we dragged his body into the forest and buried him. It would not be long until one or two would come looking for him, but that would be their mistake. Black Raven was a cunning assassin. Disposing of the horses was not as easy a job, but once they realized they were free, they soon found their way back into the hills. Many of them were just green broke Indian ponies and they were used to the freedom of the wilderness.

After five or six of their companions had disappeared, the band started to go out in pairs to hunt for food. They were also posting guards. The Cree Indians being very superstitious, thinking they were being followed by evil spirits. The uneasiness was getting to them. There was tension among the French Trappers also saying in their native tongue how the blood-thirsty Cree bastards just had to kill those "Mounties." Some of the Cree understood what was being said behind their backs and then the arguing would start. One of the trappers was shot just for saying the name of the Cree, who then accused him of talking about him, saying lies. They figured all the Royal Mounted Police were after them. It was just a matter of time before Black Raven and the sentries that Red Face had posted along the trail would spot me.

During the night, a few of the trappers had sneaked away taking with them horses and supplies, infuriating Red Face. He sent three of his best Cree Indians Trackers after them, to bring them back. These French Trappers were not amateurs; they figured there would be trackers after them. Setting a trap for them, planning to ambush them, they lay in waiting and when the Cree came into their lair they opened fire and killed all three. Then they laid them across their saddles, tied them down and sent them back to Red Face to let him know they would kill any more that were sent after them. Now we counted and there were only five left of the renegades that we would have to deal with and that seemed like a fair enough amount for us, before we could get to Red Face.

Tomorrow we will end this. That night I couldn't sleep and neither could Black Raven and sometime during the night, he slipped away into the darkness. Because of my uneasiness and anticipation of the fight we were to face next day, I got out of my bedroll and crept to where the horses were hobbled. There was no sign of his stallion and knowing Black Raven would not just desert me, I knew he had a plan. I got Mac saddled and had the packs ready to load on Casey in the event that we would have to leave in a hurry. I squatted against a huge pine tree and waited.

The sun was just meeting the horizon when he rode out of the trees so silently that at first I did not see him. I was about to say something like, "Where the Hell have you been?" When he motioned toward the east and then he placed his finger over him mouth. With hand signals he indicated for me to quickly get Casey loaded with the supplies while he erased any sign that we had even been here. He was very thorough, even erasing any sign of the horses and then we slowly and silently walked out of our camp leaving no sign behind.

I had to admire this Blackfoot Chief in the next days, learning how he and his people survived in the harsh wilderness and how they became the fighting force, they were known for. I made a mental note to observe everything this Chief Medicine Man, Black Raven did. There was so much about this man I wanted to know. I especially wanted to know why he was in

Colorado that summer of my youth. I really wanted to hear his story.

Most of the day we traveled along the rim of the mountains keeping the valley in view below us, making sure there were no approaching dangers following us. When we finally stopped to rest the horses, we still had some dried jerky left and ate in silence while we rested. Raven, as I started to call him, proceeded to explain that he had gone to the camp of Red Face, but he was not there, only four of his braves were left to guard the supplies and keep watch for anyone who might be following them.

Fortunately, for us they had gotten into some whiskey and had gotten drunk. Raven listened to their talk and one of them said Red Face had gone to the camp of the Cree to recruit some more warriors. He told his braves he would be back in a couple of days with enough warriors to fight the Mounted Police that might be following them and he would kill them all.

It would have been easy to kill these drunken Cree, but they were not the ones we were after, besides giving us away. "I don't want to kill four drunken Indians." Black Raven said, "I only want to kill one-half breed named Red Face. I want him to see who it is that is killing him. He will know he killed my wife and daughters and my people." I could see the determination and the hate in his eyes. There was no doubt in his mind that He would be the one to end the life of this killer. I did not say a word. That was not quite the way I had it planned for the killer of Toad and the other four Mounties.

"We must be patient," I said. "At some point they will start to feel safe and get careless, and that is when we will attack, but only if that Bastard is there." I then remembered that there was a fort called Fort of Good Hope located along the upper McKenzie River and it had just a few trappers and their Amish families. It would be a very easy place for Red Face and his renegades to raid. These people were vulnerable and wouldn't have a chance against these veteran killers. When I approached Raven about them, He did not want to go there and warn them. I reminded him if there would have been someone who would have warned his village the outcome might have been different.

"We will have to hurry to get there before they do, and I am sure they are not too far behind us," I continued. As we dropped into the valley below we crossed the wide Stewart River's raging rapids caused from the snow melt. We were able to find an area where the water was not as deep, but it was still up to the horse's bellies. It almost pulled Casey down with it. Raven was able to get another rope on her and between the two of us; we were able to gain control and finally pulled her up on shore.

As we were crossing the valley, I had a feeling that we were being followed and as I looked back, I could see a dust cloud, figuring it to be about a mile from where we had crossed the river. Raven said. "They most likely have seen our tracks in the mud as we exited the river and are following our trail." They were making much better time than we expected. Concerned, we wondered if they had spotted us yet. We had to hurry be-cause they were gaining on us. Black Raven said, "I don't think they know we are here yet." There was a dip in the tall grass and we headed for it. Raven showed me how he was making his horse lay flat on his side on the ground. I was able to get

Mac and Casey to lie down and as they sensed the danger, they gave me no problem. I could not help but think how lucky I was to have such exceptional animals.

In short time, the two scouts Red Face had sent ahead were only 20 feet from us, but did not detect us, lying there in the grass, as they walked past. We had our guns ready just in case, and they would have been so easy to kill. I wanted to, then and there, but I also knew the sound of our gunfire would alert the gang to our presence, and we would have lost the element of surprise.

Raven raised his head enough to see them and then he looked in the direction they had just come to be sure there was no one following from behind. Assured there was no one in sight, He waited a little longer then he looked again. We were just a little over half way across the valley. The grass was as tall as reeds and had provided good protection from view so we quietly got our horses to their feet leading them for a distance, then we mounted, leaning close to their backs, slipped through to the forest just at the river's edge, losing ourselves in the dense trees.

There were no signs where the two Cree had gone, so we crossed at a shallow spot and carefully moved up river. Still there was no sign of them. Raven halted his horse dismounted, and handed me the reins. Then crouching, he slowly and quietly moved up river as I waited. He came back saying he had seen their tracks just ahead of us. That they had been watching the fort, and were calculating how many people were inside. Raven took out his knife and handed me his tomahawk. He sheepishly asked me, "Can you throw one of these?" I nodded and answered, with a wide smiled and leaned closer to him and said, "Hell, yes, I'm a cowboy and every cowboy can throw an axe." He looked at me with a puzzled look then he said, "Okay cowboy, let's go kill a couple of Cree murderers."

They were dead before they knew what hit them or where their death came from. We high-tailed it back to the horses and then we galloped as fast as our horses would run to the fort. We heard them shout, "Riders coming in." As they opened the Gates, we rode our horses in reining them to a stop and dismounting. A huge burly looking man came from the slat wood framed building carrying a rifle, which he preceded to point in our direction. "Who the Hell are you and what's your business?" I stepped in front of Black Raven. Seeing the ire in him rise, I said, "I am Captain Aully Lawson of the Royal Canadian Mounted Police. We are here to capture the renegade gang of Cree Indians and French Trappers, who are with a half breed Indian known as Red Face. They have been raiding villages and settlements. They raided a Blackfoot village killing everyone, mostly women and children, while the braves were out hunting for their winter food. They also ambushed and killed five Royal Canadian Mounted Police, shooting them in the back."

Turning to Raven, I raised my hand motioning "This is the Great Medicine Man, Chief Black Raven, respected visionary of the Blackfoot Confederacy." I stopped talking just long enough to catch my breath, and then I continued, "We have tracked and believe this same group of renegades are on their way to this fort to raid and I will add they do not take prisoners. You have very little time and you had better get your people prepared and armed. We were able to slow them and detain them for a short time, but they are close, and when they realize we had to kill two of their Cree brothers they will be coming with a vengeance and mad as hell."

When they were finally convinced we were not just talking and trying to scare them, they jumped into action. There were men running in complete disorder and their women were loading rifles and putting them in place on the upper runway along the forts walls. It appeared they had been practicing this for some time, in the event that they would have to defend the fort. In a very short time, they were armed and ready. The children had been ushered to an inside room fortified with heavy doors that locked from the inside. Raven leaned over to me and asked in a whisper, "Great Chief, honored and respected, aah...ah, visionary... aah, medicine man, of the entire Blackfoot Confederacy?" "What?" You mean you're not?" I asked. He smiled and stood just a little bit taller, "Hell yah, I'm Great Chief...aah, Medicine Man of the, aah... aah, entire and all those other things you said. We both laughed under our breath at that, and then we went to our horses to get our ammunition and prepare for the battle ahead. We secured our packs and horses in a spot where they would be away from all the bullets, which we figured would be flying all around. Also with in reach in case we needed to get to them in a hurry. We were anxious to get started as we had waited a long time for this moment, and we did not have long to wait.

Although this was called a Fort, it was not very well fortified. There were only eight families living inside the compound. Along with the men, women and children, there were some trappers, who had just by chance, come here to trade for the food and goods they would need. Mostly these people were farmers. Two of the men looked like they might have some military training, the big guy who met us with the rifle,

Sam, looked like he wanted to look like he knew what he was doing and then a small man named Henry came out of one of the houses and responded to orders he was given. He had two pearl handled Colt Revolvers strapped to his hip that looked too big for him. I could only hope he knew how to shoot them without blowing his foot off first.

We went to Sam trying to explain how dangerous this Red Faced Half Breed was that we have been warning them about. "We are not sure how many there will be in the gang as he had gone to recruit more, but you can count on him to have enough of the worse killers he could get." As hard as I tried to explain, Sam just scoffed at my warnings. "You have to listen to me. These are the most dangerous, blood thirsty Cree Indians and French trappers you will ever encounter in all your life and they will have no mercy.

The worst one is the red faced monster that leads them." He laughed at me again answering in his broken English. "We have had to fight off those Blackfoot Bastards for years and we are not scared of one band of Cree Indians. Raven took one-step forward at those words. I turned putting my hand on his chest shaking my head. Raven said under his breathe, "We should let this man die for his stupidity." "I agree," I said, "But this is our fight too, we have come a long way for this day." I turned to this huge man and said, "You may have had to fight Indians, but do your women and children have to die because you will not listen to the warnings? An entire village of Blackfoot women, children, and old men were savagely massacred, raped, disemboweled, and this one band of Cree Indians and French trappers mutilated their bodies just this year. Do you want this to happen to your families?" He was silent for a moment and then he turned to Henry, "Go get all the men together and any of the women that can handle a gun. Get them loaded and ready." A warning shout was heard. "Riders coming in!"

Black Raven and I felt there was something that just was not right here as we backed behind those big log doors, when they were swung open. The two French Trappers rode in looking all around as if they were looking for something. Sam stood in the middle of the compound with his rifle in his arms, as he had when he greeted us. "What's your business?" He bellowed. They acted a bit surprised at the reception they got, but they continued to say, "We were just coming back from trapping up north and saw your cattle grazing in the field and thought maybe we could make a trade of our furs and gold for some jerky and supplies. We have gold nuggets we can trade." Sam only heard the words Gold Nuggets and his expression changed, as his greed lit up his eyes. "Come into the post and we will look at your furs and gold. We may be able to do some business." As the trappers dismounted, they looked at each other and a slight smile came across their lips.

I looked at Raven the same time he looked at me, "This would be a good time with everyone inside the compound with their guard down and these gates open to launch an attack don't you think?" Raven said, "It would be how I would do it." No sooner than the words came out of our mouths then the attack came. The renegades came through the open gate and began to shoot at everyone that was standing in the middle of the compound. No one was expecting it and was not ready. As I was shooting from behind the enormous gate; Black Raven had scaled the stairs and was shooting as he ran along the walkway above against the walls. We heard the shots from inside the post and immediately knew Sam was dead and within minutes, the two trappers emerged from the doorway and were heading for the building where the women and children were.

In an instant out of the corner of my eye, I caught a glimpse of Henry as he came out of one of the apartments. Those two Ivory Handled Colt pistols in each hand blasting away. Hitting one of the trappers in the belly but as he went down another Cree sent a knife into Henry's shoulder. Not pausing, He kept coming shooting as he walked, killing the Indian. He grabbed the knife pulling it from his shoulder, his arm went limp, but with the other hand, he threw it at the other trapper hitting him in the face. He continued to fire at the renegades, hitting everyone he aimed at. The renegades did not expect so much resistance. They surely did not expect Raven and me. They only thought there would be some helpless families there and it would be an easy raid for them.

By now, a fire had started in the apartments where the women and children were. In their panic, they ran out into a shower of bullets coming from the renegades before they made their retreat. Many of them were shot and killed, falling on top of each other in a pool of blood that had begun to form.

"Where was that Bastard Red Face?" I shouted to Raven, He had sent his entire gang in ahead of him as he watched from outside at a safe distance. His men had run into what was a suicide attack, many of them dead. A few got out with just minor wounds. They disappeared into the safety of the thick forest. The fire had destroyed much of the houses and apartments, four of the children were killed. Two women and several others were wounded, but they would recover. Sam and another man who had been inside the post were killed and a couple of the farmers were also killed. I totally underestimated that simpleminded Henry. He would recover from his wounds, but I was to find out much later that he was not the simple-minded man I thought he was. It was all a mask he wore to hide his identity. "Where did he learn to shoot like that and what was he doing with those ivory handled Colt's.

The people that were there said they planned to stay and rebuild the fort, but they said they would be a lot smarter and they were for sure going to have a better way to protect their families. Black Raven did not want to wait to go after Red Face. He said, "They are in a weakened condition and would be much easier to follow." Although I agreed with him, I felt I had to stay and help bury the dead and try to get them in a much stronger state of affairs. Black Raven said he would go see if he could track them to find out which way they would be traveling, but mostly he wanted to make sure Red Face was still with the band.

Two days had past and I had not heard from Raven. I was beginning to get anxious to move on myself. There wasn't any more I could do here, so I saddled Mac and put as many supplies on him as I thought I would need. I told Henry I would leave Casey here and come back for him later, but for now, he would be more of a hindrance then anything. I would have to move fast to catch up with Black Raven. Actually, in the back of my mind I did not want him to take away my chance to kill that half breed myself. My burning hatred for this renegade was the driving force behind all of my thinking now, but I was also worried about Raven. If he were to encounter these men and be captured, there would be no end of torture they would inflict upon him.

I had been following a faint trail that led over the mountain when I saw the sign of a fight and the blood on the ground; I knew he was in trouble. As the weather had turned cold and the dark clouds had begun to gather out of the north, I knew I had to hurry. Finding him was not going to be easy if the storm hit in these mountains.

A narrow ridge running along the edge of a deep canyon was the trail I had been following. About a quarter of a mile ahead, I could smell the faint smell of a campfire, and the distinct smell of burning flesh. Dismounting, leading Mac slowly, I crept along the brush and then I heard the voices. I was not close enough to understand what was being said and I could not understand the language. All I heard was the sound of anguish and the cry of pain. It was Black Raven. As I crept closer, I could see him tied between two trees with his arms and legs spread apart securely tied.

As I lay there trying to decide just how I was going to rescue him, I heard a sound behind me and as I whirled around, with my pistol in my hand, cocked and ready to shoot whoever was there. I heard a whispered voice say, "I don't think you want to shoot me." I recognized the voice, "Henry, what are you doing here?" "I figured you might need some help and I have been following you. My wife was one of the women who were killed and I have no reason to stay in New Hope. I figure I have as good a reason for wanting that bastard Red Face dead as anyone." "Well." I said, "I guess that makes three of us and if one of us doesn't get him the other one will." He then said, "I hope you don't mind, but I borrowed that little Casey of yours. She sure is a good one."

The cry of pain woke us up; reminding us why we were here. Henry said, "I know about these Cree Indians and if they knew Black Raven was a Chief and a Medicine man they will do more than just the average torture. They will get great pleasure out of his torture. They might already know, but this rain has slowed them down." Henry seemed to know a lot about these Cree Indians, but there was no time for talk, as the storm I had seen in the north was upon us. It came in a torrent of rain and sleet.

I tried to see Raven through the dense fury of the storm, but the only time he was visible was when the lightning lit up the sky and in those fleeting moments I could see him still tied there. As I crept closer, I could see the burn marks on his chest, left from the torture they had inflicted. I could feel my hate mount as I wanted to kill them for this. The cowards had fled when the storm hit, to a dug out cave in the side of the mountain. Their jeers and taunts could be heard above the storm as they laughed, taunting him, he hung helplessly, as the rain and sleet pelted his burned scarred body. They had been torturing him by burning him with torches from their campfire.

I heard Henry remark when he saw this, "Jesus!" We had to get him out of there before the storm let up and before they noticed us. Henry and I slowly crept through the brush and cut the ties that held his body carefully carrying him to the safety to where we had the horses tied. As I looked back, there was no sign that we had been detected. The Stallion was still tied to a rope line with the other horses. He had been watching us and let out a low knicker as we carried Raven out of the danger area, but I didn't think we dared to go back for him. I knew we

HELEN KLINE

had to get Raven out of here as quickly as we could.

He regained consciousness as we were loading him on the back of Mac. I led them away and found a large, deep cave far down the trail at the end of that narrow ridge we had just come across. I figured no one would try to follow us. I was able to build a small fire, trying to get Raven warmed. Then I got out my salve to put on the burn wounds.

I hadn't seen Henry since we had left the Cree camp, but figured he was somewhere waiting out this storm. We had no sooner gotten into the cave until the sky just seemed to open up and the rain was like a sheet coming down. The cave was large enough for me to get Mac in also and with a small fire; we were able to get warm. I did worry about that little runt of a fellow and hoped he had found a shelter.

Sometime later I heard the sound of horses hooves and as I reached for my rifle, I heard someone say, "You ain"t going to shoot me again are you?" I was never so glad to hear that voice as he led two horses through the entrance to the cave. They were dripping wet. "What the Hell?" Was all I could say? "You didn't think I was going to leave this beauty for those bastards, did you?" He said with a grin. "How is the Chief?" "He is going to be alright. What about those Cree?" I asked. "Oh, I don't think they will be coming this way; I left them a little something just so they know who they were dealing with. They are a very superstitious bunch and when they see what has taken the place of this Medicine Man they will be running as fast as they can in the other direction.

For the next night and day, the storm raged bringing snow and drifts that closed the gap in our cave door. We had enough wood to last us a couple more days and the heat from inside the cave melted a small airway for the smoke to escape. Raven was getting stronger and was able to drink some of the broth we had made from the jerky. He had looked around to see each of us, as we were crowded into this cave. He noticed his Stallion and a slight smile appeared on his face. His gaze lingered on the face of Henry and then he nodded, but neither spoke. They seemed to know each other, a secret between them.

When the storm finally subsided, we crawled out to see how much damage there was. The sky was all clear, but the mountains were covered with a blanket of white. We were hungry and in need of some real food for a change. We could not handle any more broth. Henry said he would go scout for the Cree and in the meantime, he would see about snaring us some real grub. After about 2 hours he came back and relayed that there was no sign of the Indians , but he was able to bag a couple of rabbits. He also said, "The trail out of here was too dangerous for us to travel, but we could go over the mountain if we intended to follow them." Then in a low voice, he said, "But if you decide to call this off we could always go back to the fort and wait till spring." Raven and I looked at him with that same look of determination and anger. He smiled and said, "Guess not."

W cooked the rabbits and ate without much conversation. We wanted to savor every bite. We also decided to wait until morning to continue, giving Raven another day to recuperate. He was getting stronger and the burn scars were healing. We were up and ready to travel as the sun warmed the snow, melting it as it ran down the ravine. We were not sure just how we were going to get over this mountain. Henry seemed to know where he was going as if he had been here before. He told us there was a trail just at the top where a tunnel was cut through the mountain from centuries of wind and rain, where we could get through, but it will be tight,"Then He said, "When we get through it there will be a valley below." It's possible that the renegades have been on the trail around it, but if we hurry we might get there before they do going this way."

He was right about the trail being tight. Our horses were much bigger than the small agile Indian ponies and they would balk in some of the tight walls. With a bit of coaxing, nudging, and a swat on the rump they would finally relent and go through as they were supposed to. There were times when we would take off their saddles carrying them and leading the horses through the narrow opening.

Finally, as we emerged onto the ledge, and as we looked down at the valley below, we were speechless. As far as we could see, the snow had covered the meadows in a white blanket. Huge Pine outlined the river as it twisted it's way though the edge of the valley disappearing into the canyon. This was a trapper's paradise. On each side, the high snow covered Rocky Mountains, stood majestic against the blue skies.

I felt as though we were intruding on sacred ground. I looked at Henry and without saying a word, he lowered his head and then he said, "I found this place a few years back and made a vow that I would never tell anyone about it. I planned to bring my wife and live out the rest of my life here and raise a family."The sadness I heard in his voice was something I could relate to. Raven and I knew that kind of sadness. We stood there in silence remembering.

I made a vow to myself that this valley would not be scarred by the likes of Red Face and his killers. "We have to make sure he never invades this sacred place." I said out loud, not realizing I had said it. "You might be too late." Raven gestured as he pointed to the far right of the valley, at the pass where it entered the clearing. Riders were just emerging from the forest with Red Face in the lead. My heart stopped, being replaced with a hatred that marred the sweet peace of the serenity I had just experienced. There was a tension as we all stared at them, not a care in the world not realizing this could be their last day on this earth.

Red Face stopped and looked all around, but as he began to look up towards the mountains, we pulled our horses back into the tunnel not yet ready for him to know we were here. We dismounted and crawled to the ledge to peer into the valley where he was setting up his camp at the river's edge. They were feeling safe, not posting a guard, as they lazed in comfort on the rivers edge, letting their horses roam at will. They had no idea of the hell they would be facing tomorrow. We wanted them to relax unsuspecting, as we planned our strategy. We wanted them to suffer with fear, a slow death. Theirs would not be an easy one and we wanted Red Face to be the last one to die, as we watched, letting recognition sank in.

Early next morning the screech of the Raven could be heard loud down river from their camp, startling the renegades with a start. As they rose to the sound, they noticed one of their braves was missing. They ran to the sound of the Raven as its screeching beaconed them. They stopped in horror when they saw the brave tied to a tree with both his legs and arms spread eagle. His face showed the terror and fear he must have felt before he died. The Raven was braided into his long dirty hair, tearing at his face with his talons, as It tried to get Itself loose from his bonds. His screech could be heard all over the valley.

These killers were horrified at what they saw. Fear gripped them, knowing the Raven was a sign from the Medicine Man. No one wanted to go near the body to cut it down. Cree Indians were very superstitious people and were sure this was a message from the warrior Black Raven, who, they had hung and tortured. They had seen the sign left behind and they believed he had turned into a Raven and came back to take revenge on them.

Red Face scoffed at them calling them cowards and stupid for believing such things, saying, "a man cannot turn into a bird," as he walked up to the body and cut the braid, ultimately setting the Raven free, but inside there was still enough of the Indian lore to make him feel uneasy himself, he dared not show it. He was also superstitious and had heard the stories of the power given the Medicine Man by the Great Spirit, and how he was able to take the shape of any animal he wanted.

The next time they heard the sound of the Raven, fear gripped them again as the sound came from up river. They ran for their weapons, again listening and hearing the screech. They looked to see if anyone was missing and another brave was gone. Red Face ordered the braves to go find him. They walked towards the sound of the screech, slowly and very cautious, wide-eyed; their weapons in the ready. They found him hanging with his face down almost in the water at the river's edge. The face of the Raven had been carved into his chest and another Raven braided into his hair. The look of terror on his face showed his last minutes of struggle to get free from the Ravens fury as he clawed out the eyes of the brave. Day by day, each brave would disappear. First, the screech of the Raven, then a body would be found.

Soon there were only two left. The renegades were in a debilitated state of fear. They kept telling Red Face, "We must leave here. We are in a valley of the evil Spirit of the Raven, he tells us to go. The dead ghost of the Blackfoot Medicine Man, Black Raven, curses it; we did not know who he was. He is very powerful."

Red Face was also shaken by this and there was great fear in him. "This cannot be, we did not kill the Medicine Man of the Blackfoot Confederacy and he would not come this far from his people." One of the Braves said, "Did you not know the village we raided was his village?" Red Face looked at him. The brave continued, "He disappeared during the storm. We should not have left him hanging there. A dead Raven had taken his place. Now the Ravens come to take their revenge on us for the raid of his village and the torture and death of their brother. Red Face was angry now with his accuser. "You are saying that it is me that has brought the Ravens here." The brave no longer feared Red Face as much as he feared the curse of Black Ravens Spirit. "Yes, it is you that has brought this curse upon us and had my brothers killed by this evil spirit."

Rage took over Red Face as he lunged for the brave burying his knife in his chest, stabbing him several times before cutting his throat. Covered in blood he watched as the other brave ran for his pony. Red Face threw the knife and watched as the brave fell to the ground dead.

As the three men watched from the ledge above, Black Raven was the first to speak. "It is time to finish this." He stood and walking slowly, out into the clearing, visible to his hated enemy, Red Face, and then I followed him with Henry at my side.

"You have killed enough and now you will die the coward's death, there will be no honor for you, no sacrifice and no prayers to the Great Spirit. There will be no one to sing the death songs. You will die the death of the rot, with your intestines strung over the earth for the animals to devour." Red Face recognized him and spoke with hate in his voice, "You are Chief Black Raven and it is you who has killed my warriors. You are scum Blackfoot." Then he spit on the ground. Henry stepped forward and said, "I want you to know I will enjoy watching you die a slow death of torture as you watch the animals eat your insides for the killing of my wife at the Good Hope Fort."

Now it was my turn. "I am Captain Aully Lawson of the Royal Canadian Mounted Police and I sentence you to death for the killing of my son, Captain Toad Lawson, who you shot in the back along with the four other Royal Canadian Mounted Policemen, who you ambushed on the Steward River. I also charge you for the massacre of the Blackfoot Village and the ambush at the Good Hope Fort. I am sure there are many more murders I could charge you with, including Tapping Bird and my wife Running Water just because I want their deaths avenged. In any case, you were part of it. For the record, you are to die immediately for murder in the first degree. May your spirit burn in hell for all eternity?"

There was silence for a moment as it sunk into Red Face. Henry was looking at me with that puzzled look, not saying a word. Henry was thinking to himself, "Oh, Shit, he's a lawman, things might have been different if I'd have known that and it still could be after this is all over." He had not heard Aully's speech when he introduced himself to Sam at the fort.

We threw the Cree renegade half breed across the saddle of his horse and turned the rest of the horses loose on the meadow to fend for themselves. All signs of these killers were erased forever. We rode over the mountain until we were far from the valley. All the time Red Face was yelling loud about this miserable bunch and calling us names that were not repeatable. When we finally stopped and dragged him from his horse, he fell to the ground. "This is the right place for him. There are many signs of wolves and Grizzly bear and I think maybe a mountain lion or two. It shouldn't take long for them to get his stinking scent." "This is perfect." I told my friends and they agreed.

Our task ahead is not one I will want to remember in my journal, but it was done in silence as no one spoke. Red Face was to face his fate alone. He was staked out naked, with his body left to the mercy of the predatory animals and prepared for his final execution. Afterward, Three Avengers stood in silence as we looked at the man before us, cursing, even pleading, lying before us on the ground, each with his own feelings.

We heard his pleas as we rode away, heading east along the river's edge. I wish I could say there would be some kind of peace to this, but at the time, I really did not know how I felt. I am not sure if getting revenge is all it was measured up to be. There is some sort of satisfaction in knowing you have rid the earth of one small fraction of filth and madness this half-breed Indian had inflicted on others.

We camped at the mouth of the river leading to the valley below. I turned to Black Raven first and asked, "I know I have to report this to headquarters. I do not think they will approve of the way it was done and I do not intend to tell them, only that Red Face and his gang of killers are all dead. Will you accompany me to verify that everything I say is the truth?" He said. "I will put my mark down on paper."

Then I turned to Henry and asked him if he was coming with us and to my surprise, he said, No, I think maybe I will return to my valley and spend the remainder of my life there." I have had enough of guns and fighting to last me a lifetime. I am just looking for some peace in my life." I looked at him telling him how much I had honored his friendship and wished him well. "God go with you," was his reply. We shook hands and as he rode away on my trusty Casey, he looked back and yelled, "I think I will keep this little pony of yours if you don't mind. I have kind of gotten used to her and we have gotten attached to each other." I had to laugh at that as I watched them ride away knowing I would probably never see either of them again.

Epilogue

Black Raven and I had become inseparable for the next few years. He had become my companion as we traveled the Canadian Wilderness in pursuit of the outlaws and the illegal trappers and miners. The Constable asked him if he wanted to join the Royal Canadian Mounted Police, but he told them he did not think he would do that. He figured if he did, it would take away his freedom and he was satisfied just being my deputy. I got quite a chuckle out of that.

Every day I learned something new from him. He taught me how to track and follow a trail that seemingly not there, showing me the signs. Mostly he taught me how to survive in this frozen land. Teaching me to use dogs to lighten a load with their sleds along the snow covered trails. So many times, he had saved my life. I owed him everything I was and the man I had become. He was my brother and I would have died for him.

By now, most of the miners and trappers that had come in search of gold found that it was too much sacrifice and hardships for them and they either returned to the United States or they found another way to make a living as fishermen on the coast or they built themselves a business in merchandising in Alaska. Either way most of the pioneers were settling down to a domestic life.

Black Raven said to me one day, "I am getting too old to be traipsing around in the wilderness anymore and I crave the peace of the Blackfeet People. I think I will go to the Montana Territory where they have gone. Maybe I will find another wife among them." I understood what he was saying. I too was getting tired of this life and yearned for the peaceful life on the ranch in Colorado and said if he did not mind I would like to ride for a ways with him. Maybe meet his people also.

I went to the headquarters and requested a discharge from the Mounted Police. I found another pack mule and we headed south. We decided to stop at the last Trading Post before we crossed into the Montana Territory. After we had set up our camp, we walked to the post for supplies.

One of the Mounties I had met some years ago started talking to me and I asked him what he was doing so far south. He said, "Headquarters was opening up some of the old cold case files and that he was after a criminal who had disappeared into the Canadian Wilderness about 7 years ago. He continued to say, "He was the half breed great grandson of one of the old chiefs they called Jerry Potts. They called him "The Kid" but his real name was Henry Potts. He carried two Pearl Handled Colts, and was a dead shot with them." I stopped breathing for a moment then I asked, "What did he look like?" "Well he was of average size, but he looked like he was as dumb as a rock. Some say it was all a disguise that he was very smart. They also say he knew these mountains like the back of his hand. I heard he had holed up with an Amish group of settlers at Fort Good Hope in the Northern Rockies of Canada along the McKenzie River.

Black Raven and I both looked at each other and then I asked, "Why are you here instead of in the Northwood's?" "What did he do that was worth the trip here?" "Well it seems he raped and killed a young girl from one of the ranches in

Montana. They had him locked up and were going to hang him without a fair trial, I might add.

Most people believed he was innocent, that the girl actually committed suicide after she found she was pregnant. The family did not want to admit their daughter had been having a secret affair with some Indian boy from the reservation, not Henry though. The Kid was just in the wrong place at the wrong time. There was a kangaroo court where he was found guilty and sentenced to hang. No one really did any investigating and didn't care about the truth. All this, very strict Quaker religious group wanted was to clear their daughter's name of anything as bad as having sex with an Indian. He escaped the night before the hanging, and it is believed he had gone to Canada and has not been seen since. Making it in our jurisdiction now."

"Have you seen anyone that resembles his description on your travels? I understand you were at the "Fort of Good Hope when you were after the outlaw Red Face. "Well, yes, Black Raven and I were both there, but no one there by that description. We did come across a young man fitting that description who had been captured by the Renegade gang of Red Face. They had hung him spread eagle and had tortured and burned his body with their torches, and then it appeared He was killed and butchered. If he had those two Pearl Handled Colts, Red Face kept them, leaving him to hang there. Black Raven and I buried him in those hills or what was left of him. We couldn't do anything to help him or save his life. He was already a dead man when we came upon the scene. It was an awful death, wouldn't you say Raven?" "Yes, it was an awful death. There was no honor in it." He replied.

If you would sign these papers testifying that you witnessed his death, then I will go back and tell the captain this case is closed." I signed my name and Black Raven put his mark. Next morning we crossed into the Montana Territory and I never returned to the Northwest Canadian Territory.

THE END

ALSO BY Helen Kline

Grandma Ida

19 year old John Lawson and his wife, 17 year old Ingabar, traveled across the ocean in 1865 in search of a new life from the poverty of Sweden to the free land in America. They endured many hardships and the loss of three children to build a ranch in the unforgiving, Rocky Mountains, wilderness of Colorado. As the years of hardship took its toll on them, their daughter, Ida and her husband, Charles Dawson took over the running of the ranch. As other ranchers came they worked together to build a life for their families. They grieved together as the measles epidemic took the lives of many of their children, they endured the depression, weather, and starvation, but they never gave up. Then the Bureau of Land Management and the Water Conservancy came, threatening them to leave so their valley could make room for a new reservoir to be built. They fought with everything they had; finally they traveled to Washington D.C. asking for help to save their valley. They gained an ally from the most unlikely source. The inspiration for this book came from the stories I heard about my grandparents who homesteaded in the northern wilderness of Minnesota, during the late 1890's. Their love endured for 60 years. They never once thought of quitting. In my retirement I have the time to fulfill my passion for writing and the history that needed to be told of our pioneers.

Learn more at: <u>www.outskirtspress.com/grandmaida</u>

CPSIA information can be obtained
at www.ICGtesting.com
Printed in the USA
FSOW01n1440240116
16099FS

9 781478 766902